"Here any exertion is impossible, so closely does
pleasure follow desire. Surrounded by splendor
and by death, I feel happiness too close, and the
surrender to it too constant."

From The Immoralist

---

*Richard Howard is one of the most distinguished
translators of French, and a poet and critic in his
own right. In this new version of* The Immoralist,
*he reproduces in every nuance the tone of the nar-
rator. Faithfully communicating Gide's personal,
sensual style, Mr. Howard offers an important new
version of a great modern classic.*

THE AENEID OF VIRGIL
   Translated by Allen Mandelbaum
THE BROTHERS KARAMAZOV by Fyodor Dostoevsky
BARABBAS by Pär Lagerkvist
CANDIDE by Voltaire
COLLECTED SHORT STORIES by Aldous Huxley
THE COMPLETE SHORT STORIES OF MARK TWAIN
   Edited by Charles Neider
A COUNTRY DOCTOR'S NOTEBOOK
   by Mikhail Bulgakov
CRIME AND PUNISHMENT by Fyodor Dostoevsky
FAR FROM THE MADDING CROWD by Thomas Hardy
FATHERS AND SONS by Ivan Turgenev
50 GREAT AMERICAN SHORT STORIES
   Edited by Milton Crane
FOUR SHORT NOVELS by Herman Melville
GREEN MANSIONS by W. H. Hudson
GULLIVER'S TRAVELS AND OTHER STORIES
   by Jonathan Swift
HEART OF DARKNESS and THE SECRET SHARER
   by Joseph Conrad
THE HUNCHBACK OF NOTRE DAME by Victor Hugo
THE IDIOT by Fyodor Dostoevsky
THE IMMORALIST by André Gide
LORD JIM by Joseph Conrad
MADAME BOVARY by Gustave Flaubert
THE METAMORPHOSIS AND OTHER STORIES BY
   FRANZ KAFKA Edited by Stanley Corngold
NOTES FROM UNDERGROUND by Fyodor Dostoyevsky
NOTES OF A NATIVE SON by James Baldwin
THE OCTOPUS by Frank Norris
THE ODYSSEY by Homer
SADNESS by Donald Barthelme
75 SHORT MASTERPIECES Edited by Roger Goodman
SISTER CARRIE by Theodore Dreiser
A SPY IN THE HOUSE OF LOVE by Anaïs Nin
THOREAU: WALDEN AND OTHER WRITINGS
   Edited by Joseph Wood Krutch
THREE SHORT NOVELS by Joseph Conrad
WAR AND PEACE by Leo Tolstoy
WE by Yevgeny Zamiatin

THE IMMORALIST
ANDRÉ GIDE

A New Translation by RICHARD HOWARD
Introduction and Afterword
by ALBERT J. GUERARD

*This low-priced Bantam Book
has been completely reset in a type face
designed for easy reading, and was printed
from new plates.*

THE IMMORALIST
Originally published in French as L'IMMORALISTE
Alfred A. Knopf, Inc.

PRINTING HISTORY
Knopf edition published April 1970
Bantam Modern Classic edition / October 1970
2nd printing .... August 1972   3rd printing ... October 1973
Bantam edition / September 1976

ACKNOWLEDGMENTS
Excerpt from ANDRÉ GIDE *by Albert Guerard.*
Copyright 1951, © 1969 by the President and Fellows of
Harvard College.
Reprinted by permission of Harvard University Press.

Excerpt from book review by Thomas Mann.
from THE NEW YORK TIMES, *August 19, 1951.*
Copyright © 1951 by THE NEW YORK TIMES *and*
reprinted with their permission.

ISBN 0-553-10441-1

Published simultaneously in the United States and Canada

PRINTED IN THE UNITED STATES OF AMERICA

Contents

The Immoralist was finished in 1901, a year after *The Interpretation of Dreams,* and published—"so far behind me," Gide wrote in his *Journal,* "that I cannot bear to correct the proofs"—in an edition of three hundred copies in 1902, a year before *The Will to Power.* Mrs. Bussy's translation appeared in 1930, and I care and dare to challenge comparison with it precisely because . . . it has been successful. For forty years we have had a fair sense of this famous recital, why not now a fairer still? I have tried to follow even more closely, more *amorously* Gide would have said, the movement of that voice raised almost to the tension of the lyre as it fills the night on the terrace of Sidi b. M.

If there is anything immoral about Michel it is his style; languorous, complacent sometimes, yet it is a style with all the terrible energy of a man who has made it his duty to be happy. My impulse has been to espouse, never to chasten, that style. When Michel, speaking of the irrigation system of the oases, refers to the sluices which *"amènent l'eau où la soif est trop grande,"* I believe we are to take him at his word: "leads the water where the thirst is too great," rather than at Mrs. Bussy's: "conducts the water where the ground is thirstiest"—a smoothed-out rendering which loses Michel's, and Gide's, very charged sense that only excess may be recompensed, that only *too much* thirst is to be slaked. My effort, then, is to persist even further in the letter of the work itself. For Gide belongs, we now see—and how happy the prospect would have made him—to that company of authors with whom we cannot be satisfied. We keep turning them over in our minds, returning to them: all translations date, certain works never do.

Let me loiter a little on my sense here: What is meant by saying that a translation dates, and that a new translation, forty years new of a work seventy years old, persists further in the letter of that work? It is my experience that a first translation errs on the side of pusillanimity, plays safe. Each decade has its circumlocutions, its compliances; the translator seeks these out, as we see in Mrs. Bussy's endeavors, falls back on period makeshifts instead of confronting the often radical outrage of what the author, in his incomparable originality, ventures to say. That is just it: The translator, it is seen in the fullness of time, so rarely *ventures* in this fashion. Rather he falls back, as I say; and it is his peculiar privilege, even his obligation, in his own day and age, to sally forth, to be inordinate instead of placating or merely plausible. Time reveals all translation to be paraphrase, and it is in the longing for a *standard version* that we must begin again, we translators, that we must overtake each other.

I mentioned Nietzsche and Freud as the apparent landmarks by which to locate this narrative, which might as well be called "civilization and its discontents" as "toward a genealogy of morals." In the cases of Nietzsche and of Freud we have not been content with only a first translation, and, like theirs, Gide's emblem of *the ego and its own: the flesh* is of great power for us still, an utterance from that part of ourselves to be discovered and endured only by the most tenacious skepticism. May this new version—affectionately dedicated to Robert Gottlieb—be worthy of Gide's utterance and of Mrs. Bussy's pioneer translation.

—RICHARD HOWARD

INTRODUCTION

Turmoil and the Ordering of Memory*

I

Over two-thirds of a century have passed since the publication of this very modern work. *The Immoralist* (1902) was decades ahead of its time, not least so in its refusal to explicate motive or draw moral conclusion. It is a striking example of the novel whose meaning expands then slowly contracts, as inhibitions vanish or change, and as new generations of troubled readers approach; yet which never seems out of date. The drama is an almost flawless one of individualist revolt largely caused by sexual turmoil and repression, of ideology determined by neurosis. It tells a story (exquisitely controlled by the author, not fully understood by the narrator-protagonist Michel) of a man drawn between a longing to concentrate the ego and an impulse to dissolve it; between the temptations of order and anarchy, security and risk, conformity and vagabondage; between, as he comes to see it, slavery and a frightening freedom. The conflicts touch every aspect of Michel's life, even his lectures at the Collège de France. There, respectable married scholar, he delivers his apologia for barbarism and nonculture. And all these conflicts are affected by a force that, vibrating secretly throughout the narrative, is revealed in its very last line: the pressure of a latent

---

* This introduction summarizes the personal experience of repression and revolt, of sexual turmoil and liberation, on which *The Immoralist* was based. It draws on information not available when the editor's book on Gide was published in 1951.

Pages from that book, considering *The Immoralist* as a work of art, and interpreting Michel's conflicts rather than Gide's, appear in the Afterword. That critique assumes the novel has already been read. I have left it essentially unchanged, although two high authorities —Thomas Mann and Gide himself—have commented that it praises the novel too highly. Their comments are quoted by way of an appendix.

homosexuality. Michel, talking to old friends, at last admits to them what he has been struggling to admit to himself.

But this psychosexual theme was little understood by readers in 1902. They were not attuned to the technique of the imperceptive or obtuse narrator, and took everything Michel said at face value, evasions and rationalizations alike. Nor would they respond as we do to natural descriptions (or descriptions of Arab boys) that delicately project muted sexual longings. No doubt they were simply baffled by the presence in the novel of so many small Arabs, or innocently pleased by them, as Gide's mother was on her unfortunate trip to North Africa. The few early readers were sufficiently shocked by suggested connections between bodily health and the life of the intellect, tuberculosis and a philosophy of joy. Nietzsche, not Freud, was in the air, in 1902, for the average Paris intellectual. *The Immoralist* seemed to be "about" individualism, egoism, ruthless self-fulfillment: a novel of ideas. The issues raised by Nietzsche were pressing ones at a time of declining faith and threatened institutions —the ethical value of transvaluation, the obligation to the self transcending any obligation to the herd, the scorn for the weak. Some dismayed readers of *The Immoralist* may have seen only a story of sickness and moral failure. More perceptive readers saw the problem of individualism and a pagan ethic posed in unusually balanced or uncertain terms. But only a very few saw the homosexual component at all.

Later (as even a Nietzschean individualism came to seem less startling) interest shifted very gradually to the sexual drama. It became permissible to talk about such things, though French criticism long continued to resist a genuine Freudian understanding. Some readers, as Gide revealed more and more of his personal history, debated the relationship of author and protagonist, and concluded that Gide escaped Michel's plight because he was an artist and could write about it. They correctly saw the novel as faithful to a strategy, continued decade after decade, of confession and justification. Here, as in *La Porte étroite* and *La Symphonie pastorale,* Gide pushed his own convictions and impulses to an extreme, and condemned himself by proxy. In any event, *The Immoralist* had its liberating value, in the 1920's and 1930's, as an utterly serious novel of latent homosexuality and generalized rebellion. The novel, like the autobiography *Si le grain ne meurt* (1926, *If It Die*), treated its subject without embarrassment or pornographic leer.

Today, to be sure, the sexual insights of *The Immoralist* will hardly seem startling, nor its audacity very noticeable in the clinical ambiance and epoch of Burroughs and Genet. The directness of some of Michel's ritual or symbolic acts, say the shaving of the beard, may even seem amusing to our sophisticated time. (Again and again, sinuous sentence structure protects, in the French, covers as it were, an action or scene which may seem too denuded or too simple in its meaning. The gravity of the narrator's voice and the subtleties of syntax and diction keep things at a saving distance.) As late as 1947 *The Immoralist*'s psychology seemed, to very good college students, baffling and new; that innocence is now gone. Yet the novel remains a deeply moving and disturbing one: an absolutely authentic rendering of the conflict between conscious and unconscious forces, and of the relationship of repression and revolt. It is after all still possible to be repressed, and the reader who generalizes Michel's drama into any form of buried conflict is not wholly betraying the author. We can still respond to the problems of mismarriage, and to the efforts of sincere or neurotic human beings to discover authentic selves and authentic ways of living. Gide did not burden his book with Nietzschean *explanations* nor with pre-Freudian ones, and leaves Michel's problem unsolved—which leaves his book too, after the two-thirds of a century, still *disponible* and free.

II

The willed economy, the compression which forbade analysis, was perhaps indispensable to survival. Historically speaking, such brevity was significant at a time when the greatest talents were attempting very long books: *Nostromo* and *Buddenbrooks* and *The Ambassadors*. Gide himself called *The Immoralist* a *"récit"* rather than a novel: that is, a retrospective story told in the first person, with the narrator himself as its subject.* It is a genre peculiarly congenial to stories of bewilderment, alienation, compulsion, obsession: Benjamin Constant's *Adolphe* and Radiguet's *Devil in the Flesh, Notes from Underground* and *The Fall, Heart of Darkness* and *The Turn of the Screw, The Secret Sharer* and *The Aspern Papers*. The narrator, as a rule incapable of fully understanding his own story, must yet supply the reader with the materials for understanding it—through tone and style more often than through statement, through tendentious image and significant though unemphasized detail. And all the while he must convey with immediacy the turbulence of the experience he has survived. The recollected past must be a dramatic present. No form of fiction requires so much authorial control. The *"récit"* is the most classical of fictional genres.†

This very ordered novel began as something different. In 1895 Gide wrote a fragment called "Ménalque," later incorporated in *Les Nourritures terrestres* (1897, *Fruits of the Earth*). It was his first call to hedonist vagabond liberation and first eloquent attack on all conformity. The Ménalque of this fragment was little more than an eloquent voice and projection of authorial longings. But he may already have taken on, in Gide's imagination, real fictional substance as well as some of the lineaments of Oscar Wilde. *The Immoralist* was to have been a "life

---

* Gide used the term *"roman,"* or novel, only for *Les Faux-Monnayeurs* (1926, *The Counterfeiters*). The other *"récits"* were *La Porte étroite* (1909, *Strait Is the Gate*), *Isabelle* (1911), *La Symphonie pastorale* (1919), *L'École des femmes* (1929), *Robert* (1929), *Geneviève* (1936), the last three comprising an unreadable trilogy. *Thésée* (1946), a superb symbolic autobiography, might be classified as a *"récit."* Three other works were called *"soties"* or playful fantasies: *Paludes* (1895), *Le Prométhée mal enchaîné* (1899), and *Les Caves du Vatican* (1914, *Lafcadio's Adventures*). Anyone but Gide would call *Les Caves du Vatican* a novel. Gide's first book, *Les Cahiers d'André Walter* (1891), and *Le Voyage d'Urien* (1893) might be called symbolist novels or romances.

† See the Afterword for a comparison of *The Immoralist* and several other masterpieces of the genre.

of Ménalque"; it would doubtless have been a far more didactic novel than the one we have. Ménalque remains in the finished book, unfortunately–I think, playing his role of tempter, psychiatrist, catalyst. Wilde had an indispensable part in Gide's own history. But the interior drama of Michel required no such outside intellectual force (and rather artificial, unfictionized voice) to compel self-recognition.

The compression and control, exercised over years of planning and writing, are all the more remarkable because the novel is so very closely based on his own history of turmoil and distress. Conrad (in *The Secret Sharer*) transposed and distanced his own anxiety and crisis of competence by drawing on a famous crime at sea that had occurred many years before. But Gide in *The Immoralist* uses in considerable detail some of the crucial events of his North African journeys of 1893 and 1895: his own bout with tuberculosis and discovery of homosexual leanings, his oscillations between constraint and vagabond rebellion, his troubled marriage and honeymoon. He told part of the story, and made his first fully public confession, in *Si le grain ne meurt,* one of the greatest of autobiographies. But only the posthumous publication of *Et Nunc Manet in Te* (incorporated in *Madeleine*) revealed the tragedy of his marriage: a tragedy in which sexual failure was compounded by misunderstanding and a wall of silence. We now know that Gide suffered, far more intensely than Michel, the torments and temptations of the final journey with Marceline. The novel is rather closer to real life, in these tragic pages, than I had supposed in my earlier analysis.

Of the two tragic histories—Gide's and Michel's—Gide's was much the more complicated. The remarkable and admirable thing is that he was able to "leave out" so much that was compelling in his own struggle and liberation. Gide transferred an experience of anxiety and turmoil caused by latent homosexuality and unconscious repression (an experience which preceded his marriage) to a Michel who has just been married. Repression for both Gide and Michel led to generalized rebellion, and to the attack on accepted decencies. Gide's revolt had begun even before he left for North Africa; Michel's had not. In both stories the tubercular attack immediately preceded the attraction to a number of Arab boys—an attraction both men at first interpreted as an envious sympathy with vitality and health. The two honeymoons were similar, but with a change that made all the difference for art. Gide knew perfectly well what he was groping for or suppressing (and not always suppressing) during his long honeymoon; Michel did not know until near the end. Gide's actual story might have invited the labyrinthine art of Proust or Mann, and have weighed the influence of childhood, of reading, of relatives and friends. Michel's much simpler tragedy resulted in a classical concentration of form and a distilled psychological portrait of buried not overt conflict. In certain respects Gide's story is of the 1890's; Michel's (except for the 'ninetyish Ménalque) is timeless.

The menace of autobiography is always serious for the fiction writer; one can only speculate with dismay on Gide's success. In all probability the imagining of four radical changes from his own story made possible a necessary separation of author and character. Without these transpositions, the novel might well have become the long and chaotic self-justification we would have every right to expect:

1. Gide's appallingly domineering and puritanic mother was alive during his crucial period of self-discovery. She is unmistakably responsible, more than any one person or force, for the homosexual neurosis. But the part of Michel's mother is very slight.

2. Unlike Michel, Gide was anything but indifferent to his wife at the time of their marriage. He had been begging her to marry him for years; already at thirteen had discovered in her the "mystic orient" of his life. She probably remained, until her death in 1938, and in spite of the long silences and separations, and the radical divergences of attitude, the person he loved most of all.

3. The most important change must be reiterated: Gide discovered his homosexuality before his marriage rather than after it.

4. Gide did not, like Michel, end in apathy, acedia,

torpor, and not only because he was capable of writing *The Immoralist*. Instead the great sinner (sometimes sinning on puritanic grounds) went on to win the Nobel Prize, to be recognized as one of the high liberating influences of the century, appropriately honored at his death by the Ministry of Education.

The reader of *The Immoralist* needs no more of Gide's story than this, and perhaps not even this much. But the long curve and wavering lines of his neurosis and rebellion, in 1893–1895, are of such great intrinsic interest as to warrant a brief summary. The story reminds us again (but by no means discouragingly) of the links between neurosis and healing ideology, constitutional weakness and powerful protest, childhood failure and enduring success.

III

Jean Delay's *The Youth of André Gide*, the work of an eminent psychologist of wide culture and exceptional literary taste, shows that *The Immoralist* was more intimately based on the North African adventure than anyone had supposed. The most enlightening book on Gide's homosexuality, it is also a work of great literary scholarship. And of course it is pleasing to find a psychiatric critic who insists on the important part reading played in the divers rebellions and liberations. Most psychiatric critics underestimate an author's reading and conscious explorations; many professors of literature attend to nothing else. The fact that Delay has written several novels may account in part for his sympathetic insight into the creative process.

Delay can hardly improve, of course, on Gide's own picture of childhood neurosis and misery in *Si le grain ne meurt*. There was no strong classic Oedipal situation. The gentle scholarly father died when Gide was eleven, leaving him in the stifling Huguenot household the mother had long dominated, and with other saintly women in the offing. Gide's mother was opposed on principle to freedom, novelty, grace, change. One of her first acts after her husband's death was to lock his library; it was not reopened until Gide was almost sixteen. At first he was made to read in her presence, and aloud, lest any impure thought or phrase intrude. She made him wear starched shirts, forbade the playing of Chopin as unhealthy, and (a rich woman) made him account for every penny. Long after he was well launched in his literary career she would bombard him with telegrams of admonition and advice. The authority or dependency was extraordinarily prolonged: Gide was not separated one day from his mother between the ages of eleven and twenty-three.

Most prosperous French Protestant households are more oppressive than comparable ones in England or America; and horror of sexuality long remained the cornerstone of ethics. Gide's dread had been established or aggravated, even before the father's death, by a foolish teacher and a doctor. At nine Gide was caught masturbating in school, was expelled, and was threatened by the doctor with castration. Thereafter, and on and off for many years, the struggle with masturbation was harrowing and obsessive. Gide had little formal schooling, and much of his childhood was devoted to episodes of neurotic invalidism, some feigned and some not. At almost the same age and in almost the same year, Delay notes, Proust was also profiting by illness. But where illness was a refuge for Gide from the mother's severe regimen, and a flight from total dependency, Proust was magnifying his illness in order to increase the dependency.

Significantly, Gide's love for his first cousin Madeleine Rondeaux developed at the worst moment of adolescent turmoil. He was thirteen when he discovered her intolerable grief (over her mother's infidelity) and with it the "mystic orient" of his life. He determined then and there to shelter her from fear, from evil, from life; and from "a grief I would need all my love and all my life to cure." The "angelism" which characterized Gide's attitude toward Madeleine, and its implied separation of impure sexuality and pure love, may well have become definitive this early. Such saintly beings as Madeleine and his mother, or the companion Anna Shackleton, or Aunt

Claire, could hardly be supposed to have thoughts of sexuality, let alone desire sexual relations.

The piety and puritanism of Madeleine Rondeaux was far more delicate and sensitive than that of Gide's mother, her personality milder and more resigned. In Gide's books and diaries she was referred to as "Emmanuèle": God with us. But she was a deeply cultured as well as tender person with, Gide tells us, an incomparably beautiful smile. Later, she led an ever more austere and self-impoverishing life; but for this decline Gide himself takes the blame. The identification of mother and wife remained strong. Both in his works and in his dreams (even very late in life) Gide at times confused the two women, both playing inhibitory roles. Not long before their marriage we see Madeleine acknowledging her fear of Gide, while he dreams of her as an "unembraceable, elusive figure." Madeleine refused his persistent offers of marriage, and with sound enough instinct. For a marriage with Madeleine would seem to Gide doubly incestuous, as Delay explains: she existed as a mother-image, yet had been brought up with him virtually as a sister rather than first cousin. Gide's mother also disapproved the marriage over a long period, then gave in shortly before her death, perhaps because she saw Madeleine as the only person who could take up her reins of authority. She died at the very moment Gide thought he was escaping dependency at last. Seventeen days later he became engaged to Madeleine.

Before this, at twenty and twenty-one, and just embarked on his literary career, Gide conceived a regimen of purity and contemplative withdrawal. He hoped thus both to please Madeleine and to nourish his ideal of what an artist should be. He was known in Paris salons for his puritanic gravity and spotless life. But meanwhile turmoil, neurosis, and the struggle with masturbation continued unappeased. An underground resistance to puritanism had begun, within both man and writer. In December 1891 he met Oscar Wilde, and was fascinated by his immoralism, his denunciation of Christian mortifying of the flesh and instincts, his scorn for renunciation and pity. He noted that Wilde was "always trying to instil in you *a sanction for evil.*" Jean Delay's study of unpublished letters and notes leads us to make a clear separation between Wilde's general demoralizing, de-Christianizing influence in 1891 and his crucial sexual intervention in 1895. After Wilde came Goethe, four years of reading and contemplation. The battle between the influence of Goethe (so neglected in *Si le grain ne meurt*) and the influence of Christianity may well have been, Delay says, the most important one of Gide's life. This is highly arguable. But we know that on the brink of the first North African trip Gide wanted to learn from Goethe the art of giving in to temptation and finding joy and profit thereby; later, he would emulate Goethe's concern with harmonious self-fulfillment. One other writer in 1893, Ibsen, influenced Gide with his dramas of revolt against puritanism and convention. Far far more than Gide himself, Delay insists that he left for North Africa with the inner revolution underway. Unlike Michel in *The Immoralist,* he had already determined to live more abundantly. He and his friend Paul Laurens left in October 1893, with the fairly clear intent to lose their virginities by changing continents. But it was to a Goethean naturalism and to sexual normality, rather than to inversion, that Gide eagerly looked forward. "The elite of Greece, sailing on the *Argo,* did not tremble with more solemn enthusiasm." So Gide wrote, in *Si le grain ne meurt,* of their departure for Tunis.

Through most of his life Gide played complicated chess-games of the spirit, which he watched and recorded with an artist's eye. But even in 1893 Gide was simultaneously cultivating opposites. He hoped, in going to North Africa, to free himself from Christianity, from logic, from chastity. But he took along with him the Bible, *La Logique de Port-Royal,* and Goethe's *Elective Affinities.* (We also learn from Delay, significantly, that in Biskra he was reading Rousseau's *Confessions.*) Like Michel, Gide found himself threatened by tuberculosis early in the trip, and consulted a doctor at Sousse. It was there, with an Arab boy who offered himself "laughingly," that Gide had his first sexual relationship: but one so unpremeditated and even casual as to signify no lasting commitment. In Biskra, convalescent, he was charmed by many Arab boys, more numerous even than those in the novel. "I feel better when I sense the presence around me of some beautiful child who breathes." It is amusing to learn that Gide had his mother send a large package of toys to distribute to these boys, and that he had told them about her.

The great project of sexual liberation, with the Ouled Naïl prostitute Meriem, was developed in an orderly and systematic way. Gide regularly shared Meriem with Paul Laurens, and soon found his congestion and nervous condition improved. But he acknowledges (in *Si le grain ne meurt*) that on the first night he made love while imagining it was her small brother Mohammed in his arms. (Notes for *Si le grain ne meurt* suggest the prowling vicious Mohammed was the prototype for Moktir as well as for the brother of the novel's final lines.)* It is further significant that Meriem's own body was still childlike; her cynicism and savagery, moreover, obviated any dreaded fusion of sexuality and love. Would the effort to "normalize" have succeeded in the end? In any event it was brutally arrested by the arrival of Gide's mother on the scene. Gide courageously acknowledged the relationship, but accepted her immediate prohibition. His next attempt, clandestine and "far from the hotel," with Meriem's cousin En Barka, ended in fiasco. Meanwhile the mother was pleased to see Gide in the safe companionship of small Arab boys.

Gide returned to France, where he was again refused by Madeleine. Jean Delay argues that Gide knew the second trip to North Africa, in January 1895, meant a final surrender or commitment to homosexuality. In Marseilles, on the brink of departure, he wants his mother and Madeleine to go with him; he writes to his mother that he is ready to acknowledge Madeleine's authority and is "determined never to go against it." But they did not come, and in due time the famous meeting with Oscar Wilde and Lord Douglas occurred, and the episode of the cafe in Algiers. It was the response to Wilde's

---

* We see Pierre Louÿs, the writer, come to Africa to see and enjoy the fabulous Meriem, as Ménalque in the novel will interview Moktir.

question, "with what a strangled voice," that he did want the little musician, that was psychologically definitive. He had admitted to a proselytizer who was also a famous and admired writer that he *was* homosexual; self-recognition was at last achieved.

The epilogue, the unfulfilled honeymoon and tortured marriage, is best told by Gide himself, in the sad, contrite, beautiful *Et Nunc Manet in Te* (in *Madeleine*), though Jean Delay makes it clearer than Gide did that he intended a normal marriage. A doctor told him he would be capable of sexual relations; moreover, he wanted to be reassured about the children of first cousins. But the angelic mother-sister image, the inhibitory and unembraceable figure of his dreams, left him impotent. In the long retrospect of *Et Nunc Manet in Te,* a "letter to his dead wife," Gide most of all regrets that he did not make it clearer to Madeleine that his failure was through no fault of hers or lack of charm. He realized too late that she could hardly be "satisfied with discarnate love" or with a childless marriage, and he takes a large measure of blame for her gradual self-punishment and withdrawal. The most poignant note of all is that the problem was apparently never discussed. Gide says he wrote a number of his books to convince her (she did not read them) and that his work was but a "long plea for the defense." But over the forty-three years of marriage there was never an explanation; only, on this and other sexual subjects, a wall of silence. As for the over-all tension of immoralist adventurer and resigned pious housewife: "The emancipation to which I wanted to lead her had made a sorry showing and could only appear to her as rash and inhuman; in any case it was not made for her and succeeded only in wounding her. I tried to bring this out in my *Immoralist,* a book that seems to me today very imperfect, very incomplete at least, for it did not take into account or scarcely provided a glimpse of the sharper edge of the sword." That sword would in time serve Madeleine "to alienate me from her, lopping off from herself little by little everything that made me love her. Powerless, I had to watch that sacrilegious mutilation. I had cast away the right to intervene, to protest . . ."

But long before this, in 1895 and 1896, there had been the tormented honeymoon that would lead through St. Moritz and Florence back to Biskra, the compulsive destination. We now know that self-knowledge (the self-knowledge Michel long lacked) was not enough, and that Gide's behavior during that dreadful journey was more obsessive even than Michel's. In Florence he had clandestine meetings with young male models, while his wife went sightseeing; on the train from Biskra to Algiers he could not keep himself from leaning out of the window to touch schoolboys in the next compartment. This once, later that day, Madeleine did speak, "in a tone in which I felt even more sorrow than censure: 'You looked like either a criminal or a madman.'"

Then the return to La Roque, where Madeleine took over the mother's role of meticulous housekeeper. The succinct diagnosis of Jean Delay seems incontestable:

The note he wrote three months after his marriage: "How often, with Madeleine in the next room, have I mistaken her for my mother," confirms these hypotheses. It was impossible for Gide to desire a woman he mistook for his mother, not only because the prohibitions of incest were involved, but because no image was more apt to inhibit his virility than that of the puritanical Mme. Paul Gide. As a general rule neurotics—and Gide was sexually a neurotic—tend to repeat throughout their lives the complex-ridden situations of their childhoods in relation to substitutes for the parental images, thus perpetuating the early basic conflict. Gide's struggle against his wife, which began as soon as they were married, was simply the unconscious repetition of his struggle against his mother.

When the couple finally settled down in La Roque, after the nine-month journey through Switzerland, Italy and North Africa, it became less and less probable that the inhibition could ever be removed. In the family environment, which had been created by Mme. Paul Gide, all the habits and memories helped to accentuate the unconscious identification between the two images of mother and wife.

Such, no doubt vastly oversimplified, is *The Immoralist*'s personal background of confusion and neurosis

The unresolved conflicts and tensions had their share in a number of later books and in a philosophy of self-realization that brought comfort to many, and at least minutely changed the modern sensibility. But most remarkable of all, in artistic terms, remains this short novel's achievement. That Gide could reduce so much chaos and suffering to an impeccably modulated novel of fifty thousand words makes *The Immoralist* one of the true triumphs of classical art.

Albert J. Guerard

1968

TO HENRI GHÉON
his steadfast comrade

A. G.

I will praise thee; for I am fearfully and wonderfully made.

PSALMS *139:14*

I offer this book for what it is worth. It is a fruit full of bitter ash, like those desert colocynths which grow in parched places and reward one's thirst with only a more dreadful scalding, yet upon the gold sand are not without a certain beauty.

If I had intended my hero as an example, it must be granted I did anything but succeed;[1] the handful of readers who ventured to interest themselves in Michel's story did so in order to vilify him with all the force of their own righteousness. I had not embellished Marceline with so many virtues to no purpose: Michel was not forgiven for preferring her to himself.

If I had intended the book as an indictment of Michel, I should scarcely have succeeded any better, for no one thanked *me* for the indignation my hero occasioned; apparently such indignation was felt in spite of the author; from Michel it overflowed onto myself; I came very near being identified with him, according to some.

But I wanted to write this book neither as an indictment nor as an apology, and I have taken care not to pass judgment. Today's public no longer forgives an author for failing, after the action he describes, to give his verdict; indeed, in the very course of the drama he is told to take sides, to declare himself for Alceste or Philinte, for Hamlet or Ophelia, for Faust or Marguerite, for Adam or Jehovah. I do not claim, of course, that neutrality (I was about to say: indecision) is a sure sign of a great mind; but I do believe that many great minds have been greatly disinclined to . . . conclude—and that to state a problem properly is not to suppose it solved in advance.

I am reluctant to use the word "problem" here. To tell the truth, in art there are no problems—for which the work of art is not the sufficient solution.

If "problem" means "drama," shall I say that the one this book narrates, though it is played out in my hero's own soul, is nonetheless too general to remain circum-

---

[1] An edition of three hundred copies was published in June 1902.

scribed by his singular adventure. I make no claim to have invented this "problem"; it existed before my book; whether Michel triumphs or succumbs, the "problem" continues to exist, and the author offers neither triumph nor defeat as a foregone conclusion.

If certain distinguished minds have chosen to regard this drama as no more than the account of a strange case, and its hero as a sick man; if they have failed to see that some very urgent ideas of very general interest may nonetheless be found in it—that is not the fault of these ideas nor of this drama, but of the author, and I mean: of his clumsiness—though he has put into this book all his passion, all his tears, and all his care. But the real interest of a work and the interest taken in it by the public of the moment are two very different things. One may without too much conceit, I think, prefer the risk of failing to interest the moment by what is genuinely interesting—to beguiling momentarily a public fond of trash.

Be that as it may, I have tried to prove nothing, but to paint my picture well and light it properly.

THE IMMORALIST

Sidi b. M. July 30, 189–.

Yes, you were right: Michel has spoken to us, my dear brother. The account he gave is what follows. You had asked me for it; I promised it to you; but at the very moment I send it, I still hesitate, and the more I read it over, the more dreadful it seems. What will you think of our friend? Moreover, what did I think of him myself? Are we simply to condemn him, rejecting as useless capacities which give evidence of such cruelty? —But more than one man today, I fear, would venture to recognize himself in this narrative. Can we accommodate so much intelligence, so much strength—or must we refuse them any place among us?

How can a man like Michel serve the state? I confess I do not know . . . He must have an occupation. Will the high position your great merits have gained you and the power you hold permit you to find it? —You must move fast. Michel is a dedicated man—still; soon he will no longer be so, except to himself.

I am writing you beneath a flawless sky; for the twelve days Denis, Daniel and I have been here, not a cloud, not one wisp of haze. Michel says that the sky has been clear for two months.

I am neither sad nor gay; the air here fills you with a vague exaltation, induces a state which seems as remote from gaiety as it is from suffering; perhaps that is happiness.

We are staying with Michel; none of us wants to leave him; you will understand why, once you have read these pages; so it is here, in this house, that we will await your answer; do not delay.

You know what an old friendship, strong even at school but closer year after year, bound Michel to Denis, to Daniel, to me. The four of us had formed a kind of pact;

1

whenever one of us called for help, the other three would answer. So when I received that mysterious summons from Michel, I immediately notified Daniel and Denis, and the three of us, dropping everything, set out.

We had not seen Michel for three years. He had married, had been traveling with his wife, and, during his last stay in Paris, Denis was in Greece, Daniel in Russia and I, as you know, obliged to remain at our father's bedside. And though we had heard some news of him, the reports from Silas and Will, who had seen Michel in the interim, could only amaze us. A change had occurred which we could not yet explain. He was no longer the learned Puritan of the old days, the Michel whose gestures were clumsy in their very earnestness, whose gaze was so guileless that our loose talk often ceased in his presence. He was . . . but why suggest already what his own narrative will tell you?

I send you this account, then, as Denis, Daniel and I heard it. Michel delivered it on his terrace, where we were stretched out near him in the darkness, under the bright stars. By the time he had finished, day had broken over the plain. Michel's house overlooks it and the nearby village as well. In the heat, and with all the reaping done, this plain looks like the desert.

Michel's house, though simple and strange, is delightful. In winter it would be uncomfortable, for there is no glass in the windows; rather, there are no windows at all, merely huge holes in the walls. The weather is so fine that we sleep out of doors, on matting.

Let me say, too, that we had a fine trip here. We arrived in the evening, exhausted by the heat, dazed by the unfamiliarity of everything, having merely stopped over in Algiers, then in Constantine. A new train took us from Constantine to Sidi b. M., where a carriage was waiting. The road comes to an end far from the village, which is perched high on a rock like certain Umbrian towns. We climbed up on foot; two mules had taken our luggage. When you approach it by this route, Michel's house is the first in the village. A low-walled garden surrounds it, or actually a farmyard containing three crooked pomegranate trees and one splendid oleander. A Kabyl child ran away as we approached, scrambling over the wall without a word.

Michel received us without any sign of pleasure; forth-right, he seemed afraid to show affection; yet on the threshold, as we came in, he embraced all three of us solemnly.

Until nightfall, we did not exchange ten words. An almost Spartan dinner was ready in the main room, whose sumptuous decorations surprised us, but Michel's account will explain that. Then he served coffee, which he insisted on making for us. Afterward, we went up to the terrace, the view from which stretches away endlessly, and the three of us, like Job's three friends, waited there, admiring across the fiery plain the sudden decline of the day.

When it was night, Michel said:

PART ONE

My dear friends, I knew you were faithful. At my request you came to me at once, just as I should have come to you. Yet it is three years since you have seen me. May your friendship, so resistant to absence, resist as well the accounting I am about to make. For if I summoned you abruptly and made you travel to the out-of-the-way place where I live, it was solely that I might see you, that you might hear me. That is all the help I need: to speak to you. For I am at a moment in my life past which I can no longer see my way. Yet this is not exhaustion. The point is, I no longer understand. I need . . . I need to speak, I tell you. The capacity to get free is nothing; the capacity to be free, that is the task. —Let me talk about myself; I shall tell you my life, simply, without modesty and without pride, more simply than if I were speaking to myself. Listen to me:

The last time we saw each other, it was near Angers, I remember, in the little country church where I was being married. There were very few people, but the intimacy of the friends present made the commonplace ceremony into a touching one. It seemed to me that others were moved, and that moved me as well. We left the church and gathered in the house of the woman who had just become my wife; then a carriage that had been ordered drove the two of us off, according to the custom which connects, in our minds, the notion of a wedding with the vision of a railway platform.

I knew my wife very little and I supposed, without minding it too much, that she knew me no better. I had married her without loving her, mostly to please my father who, on his deathbed, was wracked by the thought of leaving me alone. I loved my father dearly; preoccupied by his suffering, I thought of nothing, those sad days, but making his last moments easier; and so I pledged my life without knowing what life could be. Our deathbed engagement was an unsmiling one, but not without a somber joy, so great was the peace it afforded my father. If I did not love my fiancée, as I say, at least I

5

had never loved any other woman. That was enough, I assumed, to insure our happiness; and though I knew nothing about myself as yet, I believed I was giving her my whole being. She was an orphan as well, and lived with her two brothers. Marceline was just twenty; I was four years older.

I said I did not love her; at least I felt for her nothing of what is called love, yet I did love her if love means tenderness, a kind of pity, as well as a good deal of respect. She was a Catholic, I am a Protestant . . . but such a tentative one! The priest accepted me, I accepted the priest. Matters were arranged easily enough.

My father was what is called an "atheist"; at least so I suppose, prevented as I was from discussing his beliefs with him by a kind of insurmountable reticence which I suspect he shared. My mother's stern Huguenot teachings had slowly faded, with her lovely image, from my heart; you know how young I was when I lost her. I did not yet suspect how great an influence that childhood morality exerts upon us, nor what mental habits it forms. That austerity for which my mother had given me a taste by indoctrinating me from the start with its principles I applied fervently to my studies. I was fifteen when my mother died; my father reared me, sustained me, devoted all his passion to my education. I was already familiar with Latin and Greek; from him I soon learned Hebrew, Sanskrit, and even Persian and Arabic. By the age of twenty, I was so advanced that he allowed me to collaborate with him. He enjoyed claiming I was his equal, and wanted to prove it to me. The *Essay on Phrygian Religious Customs,* published under his name, was my work; he had scarcely read it through; nothing brought him so much praise. He was delighted, though I was embarrassed by the success of this hoax. But I was launched on my career. The most learned scholars treated me as their colleague. I smile now at all the deference that was paid me . . . And so I turned twenty-five, having looked at almost nothing but ruins or books, and knowing nothing about life; I lavished on my work a remarkable fervor. I cared for a few friends (you were among them), but actually prized friendship rather than friends; my devotion to them was great, but it was a craving for nobility; in my heart of hearts I gloated over each fine feeling. Moreover, I knew nothing about my friends, as I knew nothing about myself. Not for a moment did it occur to me that I might lead a different life, or that others might live differently.

For my father and myself, simplicity sufficed; the two of us spent so little that I was twenty-five before I realized that we were rich. I had supposed, without dwelling much on the subject, that we had enough to live on, and acquired, after my father's example, habits of economy which rather embarrassed me when I discovered how much we actually had. I was so inattentive to such matters that even after my father's death, as his sole heir, I did not really grasp the extent of my fortune, but only upon the drawing-up of my marriage contract, when I also discovered that Marceline would bring me almost nothing.

Another and perhaps even more important thing I knew nothing about—my own health was extremely delicate. How could I have realized this, never having put it to the test? I suffered from colds now and then, and paid little attention. The excessively sedentary life I was leading weakened and protected me at the same time. Marceline, on the other hand, seemed quite strong; that she was stronger than I we were soon to learn.

We spent the night after our wedding in my Paris apartment, where two rooms had been prepared for us. We stayed in Paris only long enough for the indispensable shopping, then continued to Marseilles, where we embarked at once for Tunis.

The urgent demands, the confusion of events in too-swift succession, the obligatory emotion of my wedding immediately following the more genuine one of my grief —all this had exhausted me. It was only on shipboard that I discovered how tired I was. Hitherto each occupation, while increasing my fatigue, distracted me from it. The enforced leisure of the crossing permitted me to reflect, at last. And, it seemed, for the first time.

For the first time, too, I was willing to be deprived of

7

my work for an extended period. Heretofore I had permitted myself only brief vacations. A trip to Spain with my father, shortly after my mother's death, had lasted over a month, it is true; another to Germany, six weeks; there had been others, but always to do research—my father never forsook his very technical studies; and I, when I was not following his example, would be reading. And yet no sooner had we left Marseilles than the various memories of Granada and Seville awakened—of a purer sky, of sharper shadows, of festivities, laughter and song. That was what we would rediscover, I thought. I went up on deck and watched Marseilles slide away.

Then, all at once, I realized I was rather neglecting Marceline.

She was sitting in the bow; I walked toward her, and for the first time really looked at her.

Marceline was very pretty. You know that; you saw her. I chided myself for not having noticed it from the first. I had seen her too often to see her afresh; our families had been connected as long as I could remember; I had watched her grow up; I was used to her charm . . . For the first time I was startled, so great did it seem.

She was wearing a long veil draped over a simple black straw hat. Her coloring was blond, yet she did not seem delicate. Her skirt and bodice were both made from a Scotch plaid we had picked out together. I had not wanted her grace to be clouded by my mourning.

She sensed that I was looking at her, turned to face me . . . Up till then, I had shown her no more than routine attentions, replacing love as best I could by a kind of cool gallantry which, I was well aware, rather embarrassed her; did Marceline realize at that moment that I was looking at her, for the first time, in a new way? She stared back in her turn; then, very tenderly, smiled at me. Without a word, I sat down beside her. I had lived for myself or at least on my own terms till then; I had married without imagining my wife as anything but a comrade, without really supposing that, by our union, my life might be transformed. I had just understood at last that the monologue was ending now.

We were alone together on deck. She held up her face;

I pressed her gently against me; she raised her eyes; I kissed her on the eyelids and suddenly felt, in the wake of my kiss, a new kind of pity; it filled me so fiercely I could not restrain my tears.

"What's the matter?" Marceline asked.

We began to speak. Her entertaining comments delighted me. I had somehow acquired ideas about the stupidity of women. Beside Marceline, that evening, it was I who seemed clumsy and stupid.

So this woman to whom I was binding my life had a life of her own—and a real one! The importance of this discovery wakened me several times that night; several times I leaned over the edge of my berth to look down at Marceline, my wife, asleep in the berth below.

The next day the sky was splendid; the sea almost flat. A few leisurely conversations diminished our awkwardness still further. The marriage was truly beginning. On the last day of October we landed in Tunis.

My intention was to remain there only a few days. I shall admit my foolishness to you: nothing in this new country attracted me except Carthage and a few Roman ruins—Timgad, which Octave had told me about, the mosaics of Sousse, and above all the amphitheater of El Djem, which I intended to visit immediately. We would have to reach Sousse first, and from there take the mail coach; I was sure that nothing between here and there deserved my attention.

Yet Tunis proved a great surprise. At the contact of new sensations, certain parts of myself stirred, dormant faculties which, not having functioned as yet, retained all their mysterious youth. I was more astonished, bewildered, than entertained, and what pleased me most was Marceline's delight.

My exhaustion meanwhile became greater day by day; but I would have been ashamed to yield to it. I coughed, and felt a strange pain in the upper part of my chest. We are heading south, I thought; the warm weather will restore me.

The Sfax coach leaves Sousse at eight in the evening; it passes through El Djem at one in the morning. We had reserved inside seats. I expected to find no more than a rattletrap; the seats, however, were quite comfortable. But the cold! . . . With what naïve confidence in the mild air of the South had we dressed so lightly, and brought no more than a shawl? No sooner out of Sousse and the shelter of its hills than the wind began blowing. It galloped across the plain, screamed, whistled, leaked into each crack around the doors; nothing could protect us from it. We arrived frozen through; I, in addition, had been exhausted by the jolting of the carriage and by a terrible cough that shook me even more. What a night! —And in El Djem, no inn; a dreadful *bordj* was our only recourse. The coach was leaving; the village was asleep; the apparently limitless darkness afforded no more than a glimpse of the shapeless mass of the ruins; dogs were howling. We went back into a filthy room where two wretched cots had been set up. Marceline was shivering from the cold, but here at least the wind no longer got at us.

The next morning was bleak. We were surprised, as we came outside, to see a sky uniformly gray. The wind was still blowing, but less violently than the night before. The coach would not be back until evening . . . It was, I tell you, a dreary day. The amphitheater, explored in a few minutes, disappointed me; it actually seemed ugly under that leaden sky. Perhaps my exhaustion contributed to, increased, my boredom. Around the middle of the day, having nothing better to do, I returned to it, vainly seeking some inscriptions on the stones. Marceline, in a nook out of the wind, was reading an English book she had providently brought with her. I came and sat down beside her.

"What a miserable day!" I exclaimed. "Aren't you bored to death?"

"No, as you see: I'm reading."

"Why in the world did we come here? I hope you're not cold, at least."

"It's not too bad. What about you? You must be cold, you're so pale."

"No . . ."

At night, the wind regained all its force . . . Finally the coach arrived. We set off again.

With the first jolts my entire body began to ache. Marceline, very tired now, soon fell asleep against my shoulder. But my cough will wake her, I thought, and very gently disengaging myself I leaned against the other side of the coach. Meanwhile I was no longer coughing, no: I was spitting; this was new; I brought it up effortlessly; it came in little spasms at regular intervals; the sensation was so peculiar that at first it was almost a diversion, but I was quickly disgusted by the unfamiliar taste it left in my mouth. My handkerchief was soon of no use to me. Already my fingers were covered. Should I wake Marceline? . . . Luckily I remembered a long scarf she was wearing in her belt. I carefully pulled it free. The sputum, which I no longer repressed, came more abundantly now. I was extraordinarily relieved by it. This is the last of my cold, I thought. Suddenly I felt very weak; everything began to spin, and I realized I was going to faint. Should I wake her? . . . No, for shame! . . . (I have kept, I think, from my puritanical childhood this hatred of any surrender to weakness; I immediately called it cowardice.) I mustered my forces, making a desperate effort, and finally overcame my dizziness . . . I thought we were on shipboard again, and the noise of the wheels became the noise of the waves . . . But I had stopped spitting.

Then I subsided into a kind of sleep.

When I awakened, the sky was already bright with the dawn; Marceline was still asleep. We were approaching Sousse. The scarf in my hand was dark-colored, so that at first I noticed nothing; but when I took out my handkerchief again, I saw with stupefaction that it was soaked with blood.

My first impulse was to hide this blood from Marceline. But how? —I was covered with it; I saw it everywhere now; on my fingers especially . . . I must have had a nosebleed . . . That's it; if she questions me, I'll tell her I had a nosebleed.

Marceline was still asleep. The coach arrived. She had to get out first, and saw nothing. Two rooms had been reserved for us. I was able to rush into mine and get rid of the blood. Marceline had seen nothing.

11

Nonetheless I felt very weak, and ordered tea for both of us. And while Marceline served it, very calm, a little pale herself, smiling, a kind of irritation seized me that she had noticed nothing. Of course I knew this was unfair, I told myself that if she saw nothing it was because I had concealed it so well; all the same, despite my efforts, it grew in me like an instinct, overpowered me . . . Finally it became too strong and I could no longer hold out against it; almost casually, I said to her, "I spat blood last night."

She did not cry out; she simply grew much paler, reeled, tried to catch herself, and fell heavily to the floor.

I sprang toward her in a kind of fury: Marceline! Marceline! —After all, what have I done! Wasn't it enough that *I* should be sick? —But as I said, I was very weak; I almost fainted myself then. I managed to open the door; I called; someone came.

In my valise, I remembered, was a letter of introduction to some local official; I used this as my authority for summoning the medical officer.

Meanwhile Marceline had revived; she was at my bedside now, where I lay shivering with fever. The doctor arrived, examined us both; there was nothing wrong with Marceline, he declared, and she was none the worse for her fall; I was seriously ill; he would not venture a diagnosis, and promised to return before evening.

He returned, smiling, spoke to me and gave me various medications. I realized that he had no hope for me. —Shall I confess, I had no reaction at all. I was exhausted. I simply let myself go. —"After all, what did life have in store for me? I worked to the end, did my duty resolutely, devotedly. The rest . . . what does it matter?" I thought, rather admiring my stoicism. But what did make me suffer was the ugliness of the place. "This hotel room is hideous"—and I stared around it. All at once I realized that in the identical room next door was my wife, Marceline; and I heard her speaking; the doctor had not left; he was conferring with her, keeping his voice low on purpose. A short while passed; I must have fallen asleep . . .

When I awakened, Marceline was there. I realized that

she had been crying. I was not so attached to life as to be sorry for myself; but the ugliness of that place distressed me: almost voluptuously, my eyes rested on her.

Now, not far away, she was writing. How pretty she looked! I watched her seal several letters. Then she stood up, came over to my bed, tenderly took my hand. "How do you feel now?" she asked.

I smiled and asked grimly, "Will I get well?"

But she answered at once, "You will!" with such passionate conviction that, almost persuaded myself, I had a confused sense of all that life might be, of Marceline's love, the vague vision of such pathetic beauties that the tears welled up in my eyes and I wept a long time without trying or wanting to stop.

With what loving determination she was able to get me out of Sousse; enveloped in what tender care, protected, supported, nursed . . . from Sousse to Tunis, then from Tunis to Constantine, Marceline was magnificent. She chose Biskra as the place where I was to recuperate. Her confidence was complete; her zeal never flagged for a moment. She supervised everything, managed the departures, arranged the lodgings. She could not, alas, make that journey itself less agonizing. More than once I thought I would have to stop, give up. I perspired like a dying man, gasped for breath, repeatedly lost consciousness. At the end of the third day I reached Biskra, on the point of death.

II

Why speak of the first days? What is left of them? Their hideous memory is mute. I no longer knew who, or where, I was. All I can see, still, leaning over my bed of pain, is Marceline, my wife, my life. I know that her devoted care, that her love and nothing else, saved me. And one day, finally, like a shipwrecked sailor catching sight of land, I felt a glimmer of life awakening; I could smile at Marceline. Why tell all this? What matters is

13

that death had brushed me, as the saying goes, with its wing. What matters is that merely being alive became quite amazing for me, and that the daylight acquired an unhoped-for radiance. Till now, I would think, I never realized that I was alive. Now I would make the thrilling discovery of life.

The day came when I could get up. I was utterly entranced by our lodgings—little more than a veranda, but what a veranda! Both my room and Marceline's opened onto it, and it projected above the rooftops. Its upper deck overlooked houses, palm trees, the desert; a lower one, shaded by the branches of the nearest mimosas, adjoined the municipal park; between them, the veranda continued around the little oblong courtyard with its six symmetrical palms and ended at the stairs leading down from it. My room was huge, airy; whitewashed walls, completely bare; a little door to Marceline's room, a large glass one to the veranda.

Here the days flowed by without hours. How many times, in my solitude, I have relived those slow days! . . . Marceline is beside me. She is reading; she is sewing; she is writing. I am doing nothing. I look at her. O Marceline! Marceline! . . . I look; I see the sun; I see shadows; I see the line of shadow moving; I have so little to think about that I watch it. I am still very weak; I have great difficulty breathing; everything tires me, even reading; besides, what should I read? Being is occupation enough.

One morning, Marceline comes in laughing: "I've brought you a friend," she says, and I see behind her a dark-skinned Arab boy. His name is Bachir, and he stares at me out of huge, silent eyes. I am more disconcerted than not, and such embarrassment already tires me; I say nothing, apparently annoyed. The child, faced with the chill of my response, is abashed, turns back to Marceline and with a movement of caressing animal grace, snuggles against her, takes her hand and kisses it with a gesture which exposes his bare arms. I notice that he is naked under his skimpy white *gandoura* and patched *burnous*.

"Now sit down over there," Marceline says, observing

14

my discomfort. "Play by yourself, and don't make any noise."

The child sits on the floor, takes out of the hood of his *burnous* a knife and a piece of *djerid* which he begins whittling. He is trying to make a whistle, I suppose.

After a little while, I am no longer embarrassed by his presence. I watch him; he seems to have forgotten where he is. His feet are bare, his ankles lovely, as are his wrists. He wields his wretched knife with fascinating skill. Can I really be interested in such things? His hair is shaved in Arab fashion, and he wears a shabby *chichia* with only a hole where the tassel belongs. The *gandoura,* sliding down, reveals his delicate shoulder. I must touch it. I lean down; he turns and smiles at me. I hold out my hand for his whistle, take it and pretend to admire it extravagantly. Now he wants to leave. Marceline gives him a cookie, I give him two sous.

The next day, for the first time, I feel bored; I am waiting—for what? I feel at loose ends, uneasy. Finally I can bear it no longer: "Isn't Bachir coming this morning, Marceline?"

"I'll see if I can find him." She leaves the room, goes downstairs; a moment later she comes back, alone. What has illness done to me? I am on the verge of tears at seeing her return without Bachir.

"It was too late," she explains. "School is over and the children have all gone now. Some of them are so pretty. I think they all know me now."

"Please try to find him tomorrow, then."

The next day, Bachir returned. He sat down as he had before, took out his knife, and in trying to whittle a hard piece of wood stuck the blade into his thumb. I shuddered, but he only laughed, holding up the shiny cut and happily watching the blood run out of it. When he laughed, he showed his brilliant white teeth, then licked the wound with delight; his tongue was pink as a cat's. How healthy he was! That was what beguiled me about him: health. The health of that little body was beautiful.

The next day, he brought marbles. He wanted me to play with him. Marceline was out; she would have stopped me. I hesitated, looked at Bachir; the child grabbed my arm, thrust the marbles into my hand, forced me. I soon began to wheeze from bending over, but tried to play all the same. Bachir's pleasure enchanted me. At last I could bear no more. I was covered with sweat. I pushed the marbles away and collapsed into a chair. Bachir, alarmed, stared at me. "Sick?" he asked softly; the timbre of his voice was enchanting.

Marceline returned. "Take him away," I told her. "I'm tired this morning."

A few hours later, I had a hemorrhage. It happened while I was walking laboriously on the veranda; Marceline was busy in her room; luckily she could see nothing. Feeling out of breath, I inhaled more deeply than usual, and suddenly it came. It filled my mouth . . . but it wasn't a flow of bright blood now, like the other hemorrhages; it was a thick, hideous clot I spat onto the floor with disgust.

I staggered on a few steps. I was horribly upset, trembling with fear and rage. For up till now I had thought my recovery would simply happen, step by step; all I needed to do was wait. This brutal accident was a step backward. Strangely enough, the first hemorrhages had not affected me; I remembered how they had left me almost serene. Then what was causing my horror, my fear now? The fact that I was beginning, alas, to love life.

I turned back, bent down, took a straw and raising the clot of spittle, laid it on my handkerchief. I stared at it. The blood was ugly, blackish—something slimy, hideous. I thought of Bachir's beautiful, quick-flowing blood. And suddenly I was seized by a desire, a craving, something wilder, more imperious than I had ever felt before: to live! I wanted to live. I clenched my teeth, my fists, concentrated my whole being hopelessly, furiously in this thirst for existence.

The day before I had received a letter from T——; in answer to Marceline's anxious questions, it overflowed with medical advice; T—— had even enclosed several popular medical pamphlets and a more specialized book which for that reason seemed to me more serious. I had read the letter carelessly, the pamphlets not at all; first of all because of their resemblance to the little moralizing tracts which had crammed my childhood; second because any advice whatever irritated me; and finally because I did not believe that "Instructions to Tuberculosis Sufferers" or "A Practical Cure for Tuberculosis" could apply to my case. I did not believe I was tubercular. I preferred to attribute my first hemoptysis to a different cause; or rather, as a matter of fact, to no cause at all —I avoided thinking about it, dismissed it from my mind, and considered myself if not cured at least nearly so . . . Now I read the letter; I devoured the book, the pamphlets. Suddenly, with horrifying clarity, I realized that I had not been receiving proper treatment. Up till now I had merely let myself live, relying on the vaguest hopes; suddenly my life seemed under attack, hideously attacked at its center. A numerous, active enemy was living within me. I listened for him, spied on him, felt him. Nor would I defeat him without a struggle . . . and I added half-aloud, as though to convince myself more completely: It's a matter of will.

I prepared for war.

Evening was falling: I organized my strategy. For a while, recovery alone must become my study; my duty was my health; I must consider Good, I must call Right, whatever was healthy for me; must forget, must repulse whatever did not cure. Before suppertime, I had made certain resolutions with regard to breathing, exercise, food.

We always dined in a kind of little pavilion in the center of the veranda. Alone, serene, secluded, we delighted in the intimacy of these occasions. From a nearby hotel an elderly Negro brought us passable meals. Marceline supervised the menu, ordered one dish, sent back another . . . Not being very hungry as a rule, I did not mind the mediocre cooking, the lack of choices. Marceline, herself accustomed to eating lightly, had not known, had not even suspected, I was not getting enough nourishment. To eat heartily became the first of all my resolutions. I planned to act on it that very evening. I failed miserably: we were served some inedible soup, then a ridiculously overcooked roast.

17

My annoyance was so intense that, venting it on Marceline, I burst into a furious tirade. I reproached her; from what I said, it appeared that she should have taken the blame for the poor quality of our dishes. This tiny delay in the adoption of the new diet I had resolved upon became of the gravest importance; I forgot all the days before; this one bad meal spoiled everything. I persisted. Marceline had to go down into the town and hunt for food—a jar, a can of anything would do.

Soon she returned with a little terrine which I ate nearly all of myself, as if to prove to us both how desperately I needed more food.

That same evening, matters were decided: our meals would be of much better quality, and more numerous as well—one every three hours; the first at six-thirty in the morning. A heavy supply of canned goods would supplement the mediocre hotel cooking.

I could not sleep that night, too aroused by the anticipation of my new powers. I had a touch of fever, I suspect. There was a bottle of mineral water on the night table: I drank one glass, two; the third time, drinking straight from the bottle, I drained it in one gulp. I rehearsed my will like a lesson to be learned by heart; I educated my aggression, aimed it at whatever was around me; I had to struggle against everything: my salvation depended on no one but myself.

At last I saw the sky turn pale; the dawn had come.

This had been my vigil of arms.

The next day was Sunday. Up till now, I must confess, I hadn't bothered much about Marceline's religious preferences; whether from indifference or delicacy, I had decided it was none of my business; besides, I attached no importance to such things myself. That morning Marceline went to Mass, and told me upon her return that she had prayed for me. I looked into her eyes, and then, with as much gentleness as I could muster: "You shouldn't pray for me, Marceline."

"Oh, why?" she asked, apprehensively.

"I don't like to be indebted . . ."

18

"You reject God's help?"

"I'd owe Him something afterward. It makes for obligations; I don't want any." We seemed to be joking, but neither of us mistook the importance of our words.

"My poor friend," she sighed, "you'll never get better all by yourself."

"Well, that'll be too bad . . ." Then, seeing how disturbed she was, I added less harshly, "You'll help me."

III

I am going to speak at length of my body. I am going to speak of it so much that it will seem to you, at first, I am forgetting the mind's share. My oversight, in this narrative, is a deliberate one; it was unavoidable at the sanatorium. I was not strong enough to sustain a double life; I decided that I would think about the mind and such things later on, when I was better.

I was still far from well. I broke into a sweat over nothing, and over nothing into a chill; I had what Rousseau calls *"la courte haleine"*; sometimes a touch of fever; often, from morning on, a feeling of dreadful weariness, and then I would collapse in an armchair, indifferent to everything, self-absorbed, my sole occupation an attempt to breathe properly. I breathed according to rule, cautiously, painfully; exhaling, I would emit two jerks which my overstrained will could not entirely control; even long afterward, I avoided them only by conscious effort.

But what I suffered from most of all was my morbid sensitivity to any change in temperature. I suppose, thinking back on it today, that some general nervous disorder complicated the disease; I cannot otherwise explain a series of phenomena irreducible, it seems to me, to a simple tubercular condition. I was always too hot or too cold; would immediately bundle up with absurd exaggeration and leave off shivering only to break out in a sweat, would take off some of my things and start to shiver as soon as I stopped sweating. Parts of my body became,

19

despite their perspiration, cold as marble to the touch; nothing could warm them again. I was so sensitive to cold that a little water splashed on my foot while I was washing gave me a chill; and quite as sensitive to heat. This sensitivity persisted, still persists, but is today the source of voluptuous gratification. I believe any extreme sensitivity may become the cause of pleasure or of pain, depending on whether the organism is robust or sickly. All that disturbed me, once, has become delicious to me.

I don't know how I had managed, until then, to sleep with the windows closed; on T——'s advice, I now tried opening them at night; just a little, at first; soon I was pushing them wide; and this became a habit, a need, so that once the window was closed again, I suffocated. With what delight, later on, I was to feel the approach of the night wind, the moonlight! . . .

But I am eager to get beyond these first fumblings of health. Thanks to constant solicitude, then, to pure air and better food, my convalescence began. Hitherto, fearing the stairs would be too much for me, I had not dared leave the veranda; during the first days of January I came down at last, ventured into the park.

Marceline would accompany me, carrying a shawl. It was three in the afternoon. The wind, which is often violent in these regions and had greatly distressed me for three days, had dropped. The mildness of the air was delightful.

The public park. A broad path ran through it, shaded by two rows of that species of very tall mimosas called acacias. Benches, under these trees. A channeled stream —I mean, deeper than it was wide—more or less straight, bordering the path; then other, smaller channels distributing the stream, leading it through the park, to the plants; the heavy water is earth-colored, the color of gray or pink clay. Almost no foreigners, a few Arabs; they stroll about, and once they leave the sun, their white robes take the color of the shade.

A curious shudder ran through me when I entered this strange shade; I wrapped up in my shawl; yet no discomfort; on the contrary . . . We sat down on a bench. Marceline did not speak. Some Arabs passed; then a

20

group of children appeared. Marceline knew several of them, and waved; they came over to us. She told me their names; there were questions, answers, smiles, faces pulled, nudgings. All this irritated me somewhat, and once again my discomfort returned; I felt weary and began to perspire. But what upset me, I admit, was not the children but Marceline. Yes, however slightly, I was upset by her presence. If I had stood up, she would have followed me; if I had taken off my shawl, she would have offered to carry it; if I had put it on again, she would have asked if I felt cold. And then, I dared not speak to the children in front of her: I saw she had her protégés; in spite of myself, but stubbornly, I took an interest in the others. "Let's go back," I said to her; and I made up my mind to return to the park alone.

The next day, Marceline had to go out around ten in the morning: I seized the opportunity. Little Bachir, who rarely failed to appear in the morning, carried my shawl; I felt alert, lighthearted. We were nearly alone on the path; I walked slowly, sat down a moment, started off again. Bachir followed, chattering; faithful and obedient as a dog. I came to the place along the canal where the washerwomen worked; a flat stone was set in the middle of the stream; on it lay a little girl, her face bent over the water, one hand in the stream, tossing in or picking out twigs. Her bare feet had dipped into the water, and the moist traces left by this immersion made her skin seem darker. Bachir went over to her and said something; she turned around, smiled at me, answered Bachir in Arabic.

"It's my sister," he told me; then he explained that his mother would be coming to do her washing, and that his little sister was waiting for her. Her name was Rhadra, which meant "green," in Arabic. He said all this in a voice as charming, limpid, childlike, as my emotion upon hearing it.

"She wants you to give her two sous," he added.

I gave her ten, and was about to walk on when the mother, the washerwoman, arrived. A splendid figure she was, slow-moving, her broad forehead tattooed with blue designs, carrying a basket of wash on her head like the canephora of antiquity, and like them draped simply in a broad piece of dark-blue cloth caught up at the waist and falling straight to the feet. As soon as she saw Bachir, she scolded him harshly. He answered with vehemence; the little girl joined in; among the three of them, a real quarrel began. Finally Bachir, apparently defeated, informed me that his mother needed him this morning; sadly he handed me my shawl and I was obliged to walk on by myself.

I had not taken twenty steps when my shawl began to seem unendurably heavy; covered with sweat, I sat down on the first bench I came to. I hoped some child would appear to relieve me of this burden. The one who soon came was a tall boy of fourteen, black as a Sudanese, not at all shy, who volunteered his services. His name was Ashour. If he had not been blind in one eye, I should have found him handsome. He enjoyed chatting, explained where the stream's source was, and how beyond the park it flowed through the entire oasis. I listened to him, forgetting my exhaustion. Attractive though Bachir seemed to me, I knew him too well by now, and I was pleased by the change. In fact I resolved to come down to the park alone another day and to await, on one of the benches, the fortune of further encounters.

After having paused a few minutes more, Ashour and I reached my door. I wanted to ask him to come upstairs, but dared not, uncertain of what Marceline would say.

I found her in the dining room, fussing over a very young child so stunted and sickly that my first reaction was one of disgust rather than pity. Almost timidly, Marceline said, "The poor little thing is sick."

"I hope it's not contagious. What's the matter with him?"

"I can't quite tell, yet. He seems to hurt all over. And he doesn't speak much French; when Bachir comes tomorrow, he can act as interpreter. I've given him a little tea." Then, as if to justify herself, and because I was still standing there without saying a word, she added, "I've known him a long time, but I've never dared bring him in; I was afraid of tiring you, or perhaps upsetting you."

"Why should you be afraid?" I exclaimed. "Bring up all the children you can find, if you want to!" And I realized, with a touch of annoyance that I had not done so, how easily I could have brought Ashour upstairs.

Meanwhile I watched my wife; she was maternal, affectionate. Her tenderness was so heartfelt that the child soon left quite restored. I spoke of my excursion, and without harshness made Marceline understand why I preferred going out alone.

My nights, as a rule, were still interrupted by paroxysms which wakened me chilled to the bone or covered with sweat. That night was a very good one and almost undisturbed. The next morning, I was ready to go out as early as nine o'clock. It was a beautiful day; I felt rested, not weak at all but happy, or rather entertained. The air was still and mild, but I took my shawl nonetheless, as an excuse for striking up an acquaintance with some child who would carry it for me. I have explained that the park adjoined our terrace—I was there at once. I entered its shade with delight. The air was luminous, perfumed by the acacias, whose blossoms appear long before their leaves—unless the faint, mysterious scent came from everywhere, seeming to enter me by several senses at once, to exalt me. I even breathed more easily and my step was lighter; yet I sat down on the first bench I came to, though not so much tired as intoxicated, dazzled. I looked . . . The shadows were pale and shifting; they did not fall upon the ground, but seemed merely to rest there. O light! I listened . . . To what? Nothing; everything; each sound entranced me. I remember one shrub whose bark, from a distance, seemed to have such a strange consistency that I had to walk over and feel it. I touched it as if bestowing a caress; the sensation was enthralling. I remember . . . Was this the morning I would be born at last?

I had forgotten I was alone, forgotten the time, expecting nothing. It seemed to me that until this moment I had felt so little by virtue of thinking so much that I was astonished by a discovery: sensation was becoming as powerful as thoughts.

I say: it seemed to me; for from the depths of my

earliest childhood there awakened at last a thousand glimmerings, a thousand lost memories. My new-found sensual awareness let me acknowledge these for the first time. Yes, my senses, awakened now, were recovering a whole history, were recomposing their own past. They were alive! had never stopped living, had maintained, during all those years of study, a latent and deceitful life.

No encounter occurred that day, and I was glad of it; I took out of my pocket a little Homer I had not opened since leaving Marseilles, reread three lines of the *Odyssey*, learned them by heart; then, finding sufficient sustenance in their rhythm and reveling in them at leisure, I closed the book and remained, trembling, more alive than I had thought possible, my mind numb with happiness.

IV

Marceline, meanwhile, overjoyed to see me recovering at last, had for several days now been telling me about the wonderful palm gardens of the oasis. She loved being out of doors, and walking. The freedom which my illness thrust upon her permitted long excursions from which she returned dazzled; hitherto she had scarcely spoken of them, not daring to encourage me to accompany her, and fearing to see me saddened by an account of pleasures in which I could not yet have shared. But now that I was recovering, she counted on their attraction to complete my convalescence. My reawakened taste for walking and for observation persuaded me to her purposes. And the very next morning, we left the house together.

She preceded me along a strange path, unlike any I have ever seen in other countries. Between two rather high mud walls it meanders almost lazily; the contours of the gardens these walls confine dispose it to leisure; it curves or doubles back altogether, and right at the start a bend bewilders us; there is no knowing where we have come from or where we are heading. The steadfast water of the stream follows the path, hugs one of the walls, which are made of the same dirt as the road, the earth of the entire oasis, a soft gray or pinkish clay which the water darkens slightly, which the scorching sun crackles, and which hardens in the heat but softens after the first shower, and forms, then, a plastic soil on which bare feet leave their imprint. Above the walls, palm trees. At our approach, turtledoves flew into them. Marceline was watching me.

I had forgotten my exhaustion and my discomfort. I walked on in a kind of ecstasy, a silent happiness, an exaltation of the senses and of the flesh. At that moment, light breezes sprang up; all the fronds stirred and we saw the highest palm trees bend down; then all the air became still once more, and I heard distinctly, behind the wall, a flute melody. A gap in the wall; we passed through.

The place was full of shadow and of light; serene, and seemingly sheltered from time; full of silences and of rustlings: the faint noise of the water which flows through, irrigates the palms, and retreats from tree to tree; the circumspect call of the turtledoves; the tune of the flute a child was playing. Sitting almost naked on the trunk of a fallen palm, he was tending a herd of goats; he showed no alarm at our approach, did not run away, ceased playing only an instant.

I realized, during that tiny silence, that another flute was replying in the distance. We walked a little farther, then Marceline said, "There's no use going on—these groves are all alike; they only get a little larger at the end of the oasis . . ." She spread the shawl on the ground. "Rest a bit."

How long did we stay there? I don't remember: what did time matter? Marceline was beside me; I stretched out, laid my head on her knees. The flute song flowed on still, breaking off an instant or two, then resuming; the noise of the water . . . Now and then a goat bleated. I closed my eyes; I felt Marceline's cool hand resting on my forehead; I felt the hot sun, gently filtered by the palm trees; I had no thoughts; what did thinking matter? With extraordinary intensity, I felt.

And occasionally, a new sound; I opened my eyes; it was the faint breeze in the palms; it did not come all the way down to us, stirred only the high fronds.

The next morning, I returned to the same grove with Marceline; the evening of that day I went there alone. The goatherd who played the flute was there. I went up to him, spoke to him. His name was Lossif, he was only twelve, was handsome. He told me the names of his goats, told me that the canals are called *seghias;* not all of them are used every day, he explained; the water, carefully and sparingly distributed, satisfies the plants' thirst, then is led away from them at once. At the foot of each palm tree, a shallow basin is dug which holds enough water to irrigate the tree; an ingenious system of sluices which the child demonstrated for me controls the water, leads it where the thirst is too great.

The following day, I saw one of Lossif's brothers; he was a little older, less handsome; his name was Lachmi. Using the stumps of the old, severed fronds as a kind of ladder, he climbed to the very top of a pollarded palm; then descended nimbly, revealing under his loose cloak a golden nakedness. He brought down from the top of the tree, whose cyme had been cut, a little earthenware flask; it had been hung up there, under a recent incision, to catch the palm sap which is made into a sweet wine the Arabs prize highly. On Lachmi's invitation I tasted it, but the insipid flavor, raw yet syrupy, did not please me.

The following days I went farther; I saw other groves, other shepherds and other goats. As Marceline had said, these groves were all alike, yet each was different.

Sometimes Marceline still accompanied me; but more frequently I left her at the entrance to the groves, convincing her that I was tired, that I wanted to sit down, that she need not wait for me, as she wanted more exercise; thus she would finish the excursion without me. I remained among the children. Soon I had come to know a great many; I would have long conversations with them; I learned their games, taught them others, lost all my sous at pitch-and-toss. Some would accompany me on the path (every day I walked farther), showing me a new way back, carrying my coat and my shawl when I happened to bring both at once; before leaving them, I distributed my change; sometimes they would follow me, still playing, to my very door; sometimes, at last, they would come inside.

Then Marceline brought some into the house on her own initiative. She would bring the ones from the school whom she was encouraging in their studies; when classes were over, the clever and the well-behaved ones came upstairs; the ones I brought home were different boys, but their games united them. We made sure to have a supply of sweet drinks and delicacies on hand at all times. Soon other children came of their own accord, even when we no longer invited them. I remember each one of them; I see them still . . .

Toward the end of January, the weather suddenly changed for the worse; a cold wind began blowing, and my health immediately showed the effects. The great open space separating the oasis from the town became, once again, impassable for me, and I was obliged, as before, to be content with the city park. Then it rained; an icy rain which, on the far horizon, to the north, covered the mountains with snow.

I spent those mournful days beside the fire, dejected, angrily struggling against the illness which, in this bad weather, triumphed. Gloomy days: I could neither read nor work; the slightest effort made me break out into a nasty sweat; to focus my attention exhausted me; the moment I stopped controlling each breath, I began choking for air.

The children, during these mournful days, were the sole diversion possible for me. When it rained, only the ones we already knew would come; their clothes were soaked; they would sit in front of the fire, in a circle. I was too tired, too ill to do anything but watch them; but the presence of their health did me good. Those whom Marceline favored were weak, sickly, and too docile; I lost my temper with her and with them, and finally drove them away. To tell the truth, they frightened me.

One morning I had a curious revelation about myself: Moktir, the only one of my wife's protégés who didn't annoy me, was alone in my room with me. I was standing near the fire, both elbows on the mantel in front of a book in which I appeared to be absorbed, but I could see reflected in the glass the movements of the child behind me. A curiosity I could not quite account for made me follow his every movement. Moktir did not know he was being observed, and thought I was deep in my book. I saw him stealthily approach a table on which Marceline had put down, beside some sewing, a pair of tiny scissors, which he furtively snatched up and in a single gesture stuffed into his *burnous*. My heart pounded a moment, but the most prudent rationalization could not produce in me the slightest feeling of disgust. Quite the contrary, I could not manage to convince myself that the feeling which filled me at that moment was anything but amusement, but delight. When I had given Moktir all the time he needed to rob me properly, I turned toward him again and spoke to him as if nothing had happened. Marceline was very fond of this child; yet it was not, I believe, the fear of giving her pain which made me, when I saw her next, instead of denouncing Moktir, devise some story or other to account for the disappearance of the scissors. From that day on, Moktir became my favorite.

V

Our stay in Biskra was not to last much longer. Once the February rains were past, the heat suddenly grew too intense. After several days which had passed in a downpour, one morning I suddenly awakened to an azure sky. As soon as I was out of bed, I ran to the upper veranda. The air, from one horizon to the other, was cloudless. Under the already intense sun, mists were rising; the whole oasis was steaming; I heard the distant rumble of the overflowing Oued. The air was so pure, so weightless that I felt better at once. Marceline came; we wanted to go outside, but the mud, that day, prevented us.

Several days later we returned to Lossif's palm grove; the stalks seemed heavy, soft and tumid with sap. I did not understand the forbearance of this African earth, submerged for days at a time and now awakening from winter, drunk with water, bursting with new juices; it laughed in this springtime frenzy whose echo, whose image, I perceived within myself. Ashour and Moktir accompanied us at first; I still relished their frivolous companionship which cost no more than a half-franc piece a day; but soon, tired of them and no longer so weak that I still required the example of their health, and no longer finding in their play the sustenance I needed for my joy, I focused on Marceline the exaltation of my mind and of my senses. From her evident delight, I realized that she had been sad all this time. I apologized like a child for having often forsaken her, attributed to my weakness these evasive and unaccountable moods, declared that hitherto I had been too exhausted to make love, but that henceforth I would feel my ardor growing even as my health. I was telling the truth, but doubtless I was still quite weak, for it was only a month later that I desired Marceline.

Every dawn meanwhile aggravated the heat. There was nothing to keep us in Biskra—except that charm which was to recall me to the place later on. Our decision to leave was a sudden one. In three hours our luggage was ready. The train would leave the next morning, at daybreak.

I remember the last night. The moon was nearly full; through my wide-open window, its bright light fell into my room. Marceline was asleep, I think. I was in bed, but could not sleep. I felt I was burning with a kind of happy fever, which was nothing but life itself. I stood up, soaked my hands and face in water, then, pushing open the glass door, stepped outside.

It was already late; not a sound; not a breath; the very air seemed to be asleep. Faintly, in the distance, I could hear the Arab dogs which yelp like jackals all night long. In front of me, the little courtyard; on the wall opposite, a patch of oblique shadow; the evenly spaced palms, without a vestige of color or life, seemed immobilized forever . . . But even in sleep you can recognize a palpitation of life—here nothing seemed asleep; everything seemed dead. I was appalled by this calm; and suddenly I was invaded again, as though in assertion, in protest, in silent grievance, by the tragic sense of my life—a feeling so violent, so painful and so sudden it would have made me cry out, had I been able to scream like an animal. I took my hand, I remember, my left hand in my right; I wanted to lift it to my face, and I did so. Why? to affirm that I was alive and to find it good to be alive. I touched my forehead, my eyelids. A shudder ran through me. A day will come, I thought, a day will come, when even to raise to my lips the very water I thirst for most, I will no longer have the strength . . . I went back inside, but did not yet return to bed; I wanted to mark that night, to impose its memory upon my mind, to hold it fast; uncertain what to do, I picked up a book from my desk—the Bible— and let it fall open at random; leaning over it in the brilliant moonlight, I could read; I read these words of Christ to Peter, these words, alas, I was not to forget again: "When thou wast young, thou girdest thyself and walkest whither thou wouldst; but when thou shalt be old, thou shalt stretch forth thy hands . . ." Thou shalt stretch forth thy hands . . .

The next morning, at dawn, we left.

VI

I shall not speak of each stage of the journey. Parts have left no more than a vague memory; my health, sometimes better and sometimes worse, would still collapse in any cold wind, jeopardized by the shadow of a cloud, and my nervous state produced frequent complications; but my lungs, at least, were recovering. Each relapse was shorter and less serious; the attack as intense but my body better armed against it.

We proceeded from Tunis to Malta, then to Syracuse; I was returning to that classic terrain whose language and past were familiar. Ever since the onset of my illness, I had existed without scrutiny, without law, merely dedicating myself to staying alive, like an animal or a child. Less absorbed by suffering now, my life once again became consistent and conscious. After this long agony, I had supposed I would be reborn the same man, and soon connect my present to the past; in the novelty of an unfamiliar country I might thus delude myself; here, no longer. Everything was to teach me what still astonished me: I had changed.

When, in Syracuse and later on, I tried to resume my studies, to immerse myself once more in the detailed inspection of the past, I found that something had if not suppressed at least altered my enjoyment of it: the sense of the present. The history of the past now assumed, in my eyes, that immobility, that terrifying fixity, of the nocturnal shadows in the little courtyard at Biskra, the immobility of death. Before, I had delighted in that very fixity which afforded my mind its precision: all the facts of history had seemed to be museum pieces, or better still, specimens in an herbarium whose final desiccation helped me forget that once, rich with sap, they had lived under the sun. But now, if I could still take some pleasure in history, it was from imagining it in the present. Consequently, great political events stirred me much less than the reviving emotion I felt for poets, or for certain men of action. In Syracuse I reread Theocritus, and realized that his shepherds with their beautiful names were the very ones I had loved in Biskra.

My erudition, which awakened at each step, encumbered me, frustrating my joy. I could not see a Greek theater or temple without immediately reconstructing it in my mind. At each ancient festival site, the ruin which remained in its place made me grieve over its death—and I had a horror of death.

I came to avoid ruins, preferring to the finest monuments of the past those quarry gardens called *latomias*, where the lemons have the sweetness of oranges, and the shores of the Cyane, which flows as blue through its reeds now as when it wept for Persephone.

I came to despise in myself that knowledge which had once been my pride; such studies, formerly my whole life, no longer seemed to have more than a merely accidental and conventional relation to me. I was finding myself a different person and was happy to exist apart from them. As a specialist, I found myself stupid—as a man, did I know myself? I was scarcely born, how could I know already what I was born *as*? That would have to be learned.

To the man whom death's wing has touched, what once seemed important is so no longer; and other things become so which once did not seem important or which he did not even know existed. The layers of acquired knowledge peel away from the mind like a cosmetic and reveal, in patches, the naked flesh beneath, the authentic being hidden there.

Henceforth this was what I sought to discover: the authentic being, "the old Adam" whom the Gospels no longer accepted; the man whom everything around me —books, teachers, family and I myself—had tried from the first to suppress. And I had already glimpsed him, faint, obscured by their encrustations, but all the more valuable, all the more urgent. I scorned henceforth that secondary, learned being whom education had pasted over him. Such husks must be stripped away.

And I would compare myself to a palimpsest; I shared the thrill of the scholar who beneath more recent script discovers, on the same paper, an infinitely more precious ancient text. What was it, this occult text? In order to read it, would I not have to erase, first, the more recent ones?

Nor was I any longer the sickly and studious being whom my earlier upbringing, rigid and restrictive as it was, suited so well. This was more than a convalescence—this was an increase, a recrudescence of life, the afflux of a richer, hotter blood which would touch my thoughts one by one, penetrating everywhere, stirring, coloring the most remote, delicate and secret fibers of my being. For whether we are strong or weak, we grow accustomed to our condition; the self, according to its powers, takes shape; but what if these powers should increase, if they should afford a wider scope, what if . . . ? Not all these thoughts occurred to me at the time, and my portrait here is a falsification. To tell the truth, I did not think at all, did not scrutinize myself; a lucky fate guided me. I was afraid that some over-hasty glance might profane the mystery of my slow transformation. Time was needed for the faded letters to reappear, not an attempt to shape them. Leaving my brain alone, then, not abandoned but fallow, I gave myself up, voluptuously, to . . . myself, to things, to existence, which seemed to me divine. We had left Syracuse, and I would run down the steep road between Taormina and Mola, shouting, as if to invoke him within myself: "A new being! a new being!"

My sole effort, a constant effort then, was therefore systematically to revile or suppress whatever I believed due merely to past education and to my early moral indoctrination. In deliberate scorn of my own erudition, in disdain for my scholarly pastimes, I refused to visit Agrigento, and a few days later, on the road to Naples, did not even stop near the beautiful temple of Paestum, where Greece still breathes and where I did go, two years later, to pray to some god I no longer remember.

Why did I say "my sole effort"? What interest could I take in myself, except as a perfectible being? This unknown perfection, vaguely as I imagined it, exalted my will as never before in my longing to achieve it; I dedicated this will utterly to fortifying my body, turning it to bronze. Near Salerno, leaving the coast, we had stopped in Ravello. Here the keener air, the lure of cliffs filled with hiding places and surprises, the unexplored depth of the valleys, all contributed to my strength, to my joy, and nourished my will.

Not so much secluded from the shore as it is adjacent to the sky, Ravello, on its steep height, faces the flat, distant shore of Paestum. Under Norman rule, this was almost a major city; it is no more, today, than a cramped village where we were the only foreigners, I think. We lodged in an ancient religious establishment, now transformed into an inn; situated at the cliff's edge, its terraces and garden seemed to jut into the blue air. Past the wall loaded with vines, there was nothing to be seen, at first, but the sea; you had to walk up to the wall in order to be able to follow the terraced fields which, by stairs rather than paths, led down from Ravello to the shore. Above us, the mountain continued. Olive groves, enormous carobs; in their shade, cyclamens; higher still, chestnut groves, cool air, alpine plants; lower down, lemon trees beside the sea. They are set out in tiny, almost identical terraced gardens, shaped so by the slope of the terrain; a narrow path runs through the center from the highest point, all the way down; noiselessly you enter, like a thief. You dream, under this green shade; the foliage is dense, heavy; not a single sunbeam penetrates unfiltered; like drops of thick wax, the lemons hang, scented; in the shade they are white and greenish; they are within reach of your hand, of your thirst; they are sweet, harsh; they quench your thirst.

The shade was so deep, beneath them, that I dared not pause there after a walk which still made me perspire. Yet the stairs no longer tired me; I practiced climbing them with my mouth closed; I kept extending the intervals between rests, promising myself I could venture that far without weakness; then, reaching my goal, finding my reward in my satisfied vanity, I breathed deeply, powerfully, over and over until I seemed to feel the air penetrate my lungs more completely. I transferred my old assiduity to all these bodily preoccupations. I made progress.

I was amazed, occasionally, that my health was returning so quickly. I managed to convince myself that I had initially exaggerated the seriousness of my condition; to doubt that I had been so very ill; to laugh at the blood I had spat up; to regret that my cure had not continued to be more arduous.

I had given myself, at first, very foolish treatment,

unaware of my body's needs. I made a patient study of these, and developed, with respect to precautions and care, an ingenuity so unremitting that I made it into something like a game. What I still suffered from most was my morbid sensitivity to the slightest change in temperature. Now that my lungs were clear, I attributed this hyperesthesia to my nervous debility, an after-effect of the disease. I resolved to overcome this. The sight of the splendidly tanned peasants whose sun-drenched skins I glimpsed when they threw off their jackets in the fields encouraged me to let the same thing happen to me. One morning, stripping myself naked, I examined my body; the sight of my skinny arms, of my shoulders which the greatest efforts could not keep from slouching, but especially of the whiteness, or rather the colorlessness, of my skin filled me with shame, and tears came to my eyes. I dressed again quickly, and instead of heading down toward Amalfi, as I was accustomed to do, I made for the rocks covered with low-growing grass and moss, far from houses or roads, where I knew I could not be seen. Here I slowly undressed. The air was quite cool, but the sun broiling. I offered the whole of my body to its flames. I sat, lay down, turned over. I felt the hard soil beneath me; the stirring grass brushed my body. Though sheltered from the wind, I trembled at each breath of air. Soon a delicious radiance enveloped me; my whole being brimmed to the surface of my skin.

We stayed two weeks in Ravello; each morning I would return to those rocks, resume my cure. Soon even the one garment I still wore became uncomfortable, superfluous; my invigorated skin stopped sweating incessantly and could protect itself, now, by its own warmth.

The morning of one of those last days (it was mid-April), I dared more. In a declivity of the rocks I am describing flowed a spring of clear water. It ran down the rocks in a scanty cascade, but had hollowed out a deeper basin where it fell, and the water that collected there was very pure. Three times I had come here, had leaned over, had reclined on the brink, filled with thirst, with longing; I had stared fixedly at the smooth rocks on the bottom, where I could see no stain, no weed, and where the sun, sinking through the water, cast its shimmering net. That fourth day, I walked resolutely to the water, where it glowed brighter than ever, and without another thought plunged straight into it. Numb with cold, I came out almost at once, stretched my body on the grass, in the sunlight. There was a clump of mint growing nearby, the perfume overpowering. I picked a stalk, crushed its leaves and rubbed them all over my body, damp now but incandescent with the sun's heat. I looked at myself a long time, without any more shame, with joy. I judged myself not yet strong, but capable of strength, harmonious, sensual, almost beautiful.

VII

Thus I occupied myself, as far as any real action was concerned, with physical exercises which of course suggested my new ethic but already seemed no more than an apprenticeship, a means, and no longer satisfied me in themselves.

Nonetheless I shall account for one action here, foolish though it may seem to you, for in its very puerility it clarifies my tormenting need to express outwardly the inmost change of my being: In Amalfi, I had my beard shaved off.

Up till then I had worn a full beard, and cut my hair very close. It had never occurred to me that I might just as well have presented myself differently. And all of a sudden, the day I had stretched out naked on that rock for the first time, my beard bothered me; it was like a final garment I could not strip off; it felt artificial: carefully trimmed as it was, not pointed but squarish, it now seemed ugly, ridiculous. Back in my hotel room, I gazed at myself in the mirror and disliked what I saw; I looked like what I had been up till now: a bookworm. Right after lunch, I went down to Amalfi, my mind made up. The town is a tiny one: I had to make do with a common stall on the main square. It was market day; the shop was full and the wait endless; but neither the dubious razors, the yellowing brush, the smell, nor the barber's comments could make me waver now. Feeling my beard fall under the scissors, I seemed to be peeling off a mask. Yet when I looked at myself afterward, the emotion which filled me—though I choked it back as well as I could—was not joy but fear. I am not questioning this emotion, I am stating it. I found my features quite handsome. No, the fear grew out of my sense that others could read my thoughts now, thoughts which to me seemed suddenly fearful.

In compensation, I let my hair grow.

This was all that my new, still-idle being had found to do. I imagined it would provoke actions astonishing to myself—but later on; later on, I reassured myself, when your being is more fully formed. Forced to live on expectations, I maintained, like Descartes, a provisional mode of action. Marceline, for this very reason, may have been deceived. The change in my expression, it is true, especially the day when I appeared without my beard, the new relation of my features to each other, may perhaps have disturbed her, but she already loved me too much to see me clearly; what is more, I kept reassuring her as well as I could. It was essential that she not interfere with my rebirth; to shield it from her gaze, I would have to dissimulate.

Moreover, the man Marceline loved, the man she had married, was not my "new being." And I kept reminding myself of this, in order to force myself to conceal that being from her. Consequently I showed her no more of myself than an image which, constant and faithful to the past as it was, grew falser day by day.

My relations with Marceline therefore remained the same—although more exalted from day to day by an ever-greater love. My very dissimulation (if I may use such a word to express the necessity of shielding my thoughts from her judgment), my dissimulation increased my love. I mean that my enterprise unceasingly involved Marceline. Perhaps this need to lie cost me something, at first: but I soon realized that what are supposedly the worst things (lying, to mention only one) are hard to do only when you have never done them; but that each of them becomes, and so quickly! easy, pleasant, sweet in the repetition, and soon a second nature. Thus, as in each instance when an initial disgust is overcome, I ended by enjoying the dissimulation itself, savoring it as I savored the functioning of my unsuspected faculties. And I advanced every day into a richer, fuller life, toward a more delicious happiness.

VIII

The road from Ravello to Sorrento is so beautiful that I was reconciled, that morning, to seeing nothing finer on earth. The warm ruggedness of the rocks, the air's abundance, its fragrance and limpidity—everything filled me with the joy of being alive until my whole being seemed no more than a hovering rapture: memories or regrets, hope or desire, future and past fell silent; I knew nothing of life but what the moment brought to it, took from it. O physical joy! I exulted, O confident rhythm of my muscles, O health!

I had left early in the morning, preceding Marceline, whose excessive composure might have tempered my joy, as her pace would have slackened mine. She would join me by carriage at Positano, where we were to lunch.

I was just approaching Positano when the sound of wheels, forming the ground bass to a peculiar singing, made me turn round abruptly. And at first I could see nothing, for the road along the cliff's edge is a winding one; then all at once a carriage dashed into view—Marceline's carriage. The driver was singing at the top of his lungs, gesticulating wildly, standing on his seat and savagely whipping the terrified horse. What a brute the man was! He rushed past, leaving me just enough time to get out of the way, and did not stop when I shouted . . . I ran after him, but the carriage was moving too fast. I was afraid Marceline might jump out, and equally afraid she might remain inside; if the horse gave a start, she could be thrown into the sea. Suddenly the horse collapsed. Marceline got down and was about to run away, but already I was at her side. The driver, once he saw me, greeted me with a stream of profanity. I was in a fury with the man, and at his first insult I rushed at him, dragged him down from his seat. We rolled together on the ground, but I didn't lose my advantage; he seemed dazed by his fall and soon was still more so from the punch in the mouth I gave him when I saw he was trying to bite me. I didn't let him go even then, but knelt on his chest and tried to pin down his arms. I stared into that hideous face which my fist had just made uglier; he was spitting, slobbering, bleeding, swearing—a horrible creature altogether! Truly, strangling seemed no more than he deserved, and I might have done it . . . At least I felt capable of it; and I believe that only the thought of the police prevented me.

I managed, with some difficulty, to tie up the maniac, and then I threw him into the carriage like a sack.

What glances, after that, Marceline and I exchanged! The danger had not been great; but I had had to show my strength, and in her defense. Then and there I realized I could give up my life for her, and give it joyfully . . . The horse had staggered to its feet. Leaving the drunkard in the back of the carriage, Marceline and I climbed up onto the box, and driving as best we could, managed to reach Positano, then Sorrento.

It was on that night that I possessed Marceline.

Have you understood me, or must I repeat that I was virtually a novice in all that has to do with love? Perhaps it was to its novelty that our wedding night owed its grace. For it seems to me, recalling it today, that that first night was the only one—so greatly did the anticipation and the surprise of love add to its pleasures; so sufficient is a single night for the utterance of the greatest love; and so stubbornly does my memory revive only that one night. It was a momentary laughter, in which our souls united. But I think there comes a point in love, a unique moment which later on the soul seeks in vain to surpass, and that the effort to revive such happiness depletes it; that nothing thwarts happiness so much as the memory of happiness. Alas! I remember that night.

Our hotel was outside the town, surrounded by gardens,

by orchards; our room opened onto a wide balcony; branches brushed against it. Dawn entered freely through our wide-open windows. I got up in silence and leaned tenderly over Marceline. She was asleep, and appeared to be smiling in her sleep. It seemed to me, now that I was stronger, that she had become even more delicate, as if all her grace were a kind of fragility. Tumultuous thoughts whirled through my mind. I realized she was telling the truth when she said that I meant everything to her; and my next thought was: what am I doing for her happiness? I abandon her almost the whole of every day; she expects everything of me, and I forsake her—poor Marceline! Tears filled my eyes. Vainly I ransacked my past debility for an excuse: what need had I now of her constant care and of my selfishness? Was I not stronger than she at this moment?

The smile had left her cheeks; dawn, though gilding everything, revealed her to me suddenly sad and wan —and perhaps the morning's approach awakened my anxiety. I challenged myself: must I some day, in my turn, take care of you, worry about you, Marceline? I shuddered; and overcome with love, with pity, with tenderness, I gently rested my lips between her closed eyes in the tenderest, the most loving and the most reverent of kisses.

IX

The few days we spent in Sorrento were smiling days, somnolent ones. Had I ever enjoyed such calm, such content? Would I enjoy their like again? . . . I was with Marceline unceasingly; paying less attention to myself and more to her, I found in our conversations the pleasure I had taken, the days before, in my silence.

I was amazed at first to learn that our wandering life, which I claimed to find so satisfying, appealed to her only as a temporary condition; but all at once the idleness of such an existence became apparent to me, and I acknowledged that it was only a phase; for the first time, a desire to work born of the very leisure granted at last by my recovery, I spoke seriously of going home; from Marceline's joy at my words, I realized she had been dreaming of this for a long time.

Yet the various historical studies I began reconsidering no longer afforded me the same pleasure. I've told you: since my illness, all abstract and neutral knowledge of the past had seemed futile to me, and if not so long ago I might have undertaken philological research, applying myself, for instance, to determining the Goths' responsibility in the corruption of the Latin language, and neglecting, misunderstanding such figures as Theodoric, Cassiodorus, Amalaswintha and their splendid passions for the sake of mere signs, the residue of their lives; now these same signs, and philology as a whole, were no more to me than another means of penetrating deeper into a subject whose barbaric grandeur and nobility had just become evident. I decided to consider this period more closely, to limit myself for a while to the final years of the empire of the Goths, and to take advantage of our imminent visit to Ravenna, the scene of its death throes.

But, I must admit, the figure of the young king Athalaric was what attracted me most to the subject. I imagined this fifteen-year-old, covertly spurred on by the Goths, rebelling against his mother Amalaswintha, balking at his Latin education, rejecting culture like a stallion restive in harness and, preferring the company of the tumultuous Goths to that of the old and over-prudent Cassiodorus, enjoying for a few years with unruly favorites his own age a violent, voluptuous, unbridled life, dying at eighteen, utterly corrupted, glutted with debauchery. I recognized in this tragic thirst for a wilder and unspoiled existence something of what Marceline used to call, with a smile, my "attack." I sought relief by applying to it at least my mind, since my body was no longer concerned, and I did my best to convince myself there was a lesson to be read in Athalaric's hideous death.

Before Ravenna, then, where we would stay for two weeks, we would do a little sightseeing in Rome and Florence, and by leaving out Venice and Verona would shorten the end of our trip, not stopping again until we reached Paris. I discovered an entirely new pleasure in discussing the future with Marceline; some uncertainty still remained about our summer plans; both of us were tired of traveling and had no desire to set out again; I wanted complete calm for my studies; and we thought of the farm between Lisieux and Pont-l'Évêque, in the greenest part of Normandy—an estate that once belonged to my mother, where I had spent several of my childhood summers with her, but to which I had not returned since her death. My father had entrusted its management to a bailiff, now an old man, who collected the rents and sent them to us regularly. The large and very pleasant house, in a garden crisscrossed with running streams, had left me with magical memories; the place was called La Morinière; it seemed to me it would be a good place to live.

I mentioned the possibility of spending the following winter in Rome; as a worker, this time, no longer as a tourist. But this latest plan was quickly altered: in the pile of mail which had long been waiting for us in Naples, one letter unexpectedly reported that when a chair at the Collège de France had fallen vacant, my name had been proposed several times; it was only an interim appointment, but one which, for that very reason, would leave me more freedom in the future; my informant suggested the various steps to be taken, if I were interested, and strongly advised me to accept. I hesitated, regarding the post, at first, as no more than a kind of bondage; then I decided it might be interesting to present, in a series of lectures, my work on Cassiodorus. The pleasure I would be giving Marceline managed to convince me. And once my decision was made, I saw only its advantages.

In the scholarly circles of Rome and Florence, my father maintained various connections with whom I myself had entered into correspondence. They afforded me every means of making whatever investigations I wished, in Ravenna and elsewhere; I no longer thought of anything except my work. Marceline found a thousand charming ways to further my project by her countless attentions.

Our happiness, during this last part of the trip, was

so untroubled, so calm, that I have nothing to tell about it. The loveliest creations of men are persistently painful. What would be the description of happiness? Nothing, except what prepares and then what destroys it, can be told. —And now I have told you all that had prepared it.

PART TWO

We arrived at La Morinière the first days of July, having stayed in Paris only long enough to pay a brief round of visits and to send on provisions.

La Morinière, I have told you, is situated between Lisieux and Pont-l'Évêque, in the shadiest, wettest countryside I know. Countless gently curving foothills slope down to the broad Auge valley, which suddenly flattens out as it approaches the sea. No horizon; woods full of mystery; a few plowed fields, but mostly meadows, hilly pasturage where the thick grass is mowed twice a year, where the many apple trees mingle their shadows when the sun is low, where the herds graze untended; in each hollow, water: pond, pool or stream; you hear a continual trickling.

How well I remembered the house! its blue roofs, its brick and stone walls, its moats, the reflections in the sleeping water . . . It was an old house where we could have lodged more than a dozen; Marceline, three servants, myself occasionally helping, had all we could do to enliven one wing. Our old caretaker, whose name was Bocage, had already had some of the rooms made ready as best he could: the old furniture was awakened from its sleep of twenty years, everything had remained just as my memory saw it, the paneling not too ramshackle, the rooms easily habitable. To welcome us more festively Bocage had filled all the vases he had found with flowers. He had had the courtyard and the paths nearest the house weeded and raked. When we arrived the house was glowing in the sun's last beams, and out of the valley before it had risen a motionless mist which veiled and revealed the river. Even before we arrived I suddenly recognized the smell of the grass; and when I heard, once again, the shrill cries of the swallows circling the house, all the past suddenly rose up as if it had been waiting for me and, recognizing me, sought to envelop my approach.

Within a few days the house became almost comfortable; I could have begun my work; I delayed, still listening as my past reminded me of itself, detail by detail, and soon after occupied by an emotion all too new: Mar-

44

celine, a week after our arrival, confided that she was pregnant.

It seemed to me henceforth that I owed her a new care, that she was entitled to more tenderness; certainly in the period immediately after her disclosure I spent almost every moment of the day with her. We would go out and sit near the woods, on the bench where I once used to sit with my mother; here each moment came more voluptuously, each hour passed more imperceptibly. If no distinct recollection stands out from this period of my life, it is not because I am any the less grateful for it— but because everything in it mingled, dissolved into a consistent well-being, in which night melted into morning and the days were yoked to the days.

Gradually I took up my work again, my mind calm, alert, sure of its powers, regarding the future confidently and coolly, my will apparently chastened, apparently heeding the counsel of that temperate earth.

No doubt about it, I decided, the example of that earth, where everything is preparing for fruition, for the good harvest, must have the best influence upon me. I marveled at the serene future promised by those robust oxen, those fat cows in their opulent pastures. The apple trees planted in rows on the favorable hillsides heralded a splendid crop that summer; I dreamed of the rich burden of fruit beneath which their branches would soon be bending. From this orderly abundance, from this happy subservience, from this smiling cultivation, a harmony was being wrought, no longer fortuitous but imposed, a rhythm, a beauty at once human and natural, in which one could no longer tell what was most admirable, so intimately united into a perfect understanding were the fecund explosion of free nature and man's skillful effort to order it. What would that effort be, I thought, without the powerful savagery it masters? What would be the savage energy of that overflowing sap without the intelligent effort which channels and discharges it, laughing, into profusion? —And I let myself dream of such lands where every force was so well controlled, every expenditure so compensated, every exchange so strict, that the slightest waste became evident; then, applying my dream to life, I sketched an ethic which would become a science of self-exploitation perfected by a disciplined intelligence.

Where had it gone, then, my old turmoil, where was it hiding? I felt so serene now that it might never have existed. The flood tide of my love had closed over it all.

Meanwhile old Bocage made a great show of zeal around us; he gave orders, advice, lectures; we were only too aware of his need to seem indispensable. In order not to offend him, I had to examine his accounts, listen to all his endless explanations. Even that was not enough; I was forced to accompany him around the estate. His sententious platitudes, his continual preaching, his obvious self-satisfaction and paraded honesty soon managed to exasperate me; he became increasingly insistent, and I would have employed any means to regain my leisure—when an unexpected event occurred, giving my relations with him a different character: one evening Bocage announced he was expecting his son Charles the next day.

I said, "Oh yes," almost indifferently, having taken little interest hitherto in whatever children Bocage might have; then, seeing that my indifference affected him, that he was expecting some sign of interest and surprise from me, I asked, "Where has he been all this time?"

"On an experimental farm, near Alençon."

"By now he must be nearly . . ." I continued, calculating the age of this son whose very existence I had never suspected, and speaking slowly enough to leave him time to interrupt me.

"Going on eighteen," Bocage broke in. "He wasn't much more than four when Madame your mother died. Oh, he's a big fellow now; soon he'll know more than his father." And once Bocage had started, nothing could stop him again, however apparent my boredom might be.

The next day I thought no more about it until late in the afternoon, when Charles came to pay his respects to Marceline and me. He was a strapping, handsome boy, so rich in health, so supple and well built that even the dreadful city clothes he had put on in our honor could not spoil his looks; his shyness added little or nothing to his fine, high color. He seemed no more than fifteen, so childlike had the look in his eyes remained; he expressed

46

himself quite easily, without false modesty, and unlike his father spoke only when he had something to say. I don't remember what remarks we exchanged that first evening; I was so busy watching him I found nothing to say, and let Marceline do the talking. But the next day, for the first time, I did not wait for old Bocage's arrival to walk up to the farm, where I knew work had begun on the pond.

This pond, the size of a small lake, was leaking; the leak had been found, and the spot had to be cemented. In order to do this the water was being drained for the first time in fifteen years. The pond was full of carp and tench, some very large, which never left the deepest parts. I was eager to stock our moat with these, and to give some to the workmen, so that on this occasion the work was turned into a fishing party; the whole farm was alive with excitement; some neighborhood children had come, mingling with the workmen. Marceline would join us later on herself.

The water level had already been sinking a long while by the time I arrived. Occasionally a great shudder ran over the surface, and the brown backs of the disturbed fish appeared. In puddles around the edges, wading children gathered a gleaming catch which they tossed into buckets of clear water. The pond, which the terror of the fish had thoroughly muddied, grew darker from moment to moment. There were more fish than anyone could have hoped; four farmers pulled them out by the handfuls. I was sorry Marceline had not yet appeared, and was about to run back and get her when several screams announced the first eels. No one could catch them; they slid between the men's fingers. Charles, who till then had remained with his father on the bank, restrained himself no longer; he stripped off shoes, socks, jacket and vest, and then, rolling high his trousers and shirtsleeves, stepped determinedly into the mud. I followed right after.

"Well, Charles," I called, "are you glad you came home yesterday?"

He made no reply, but glanced at me, laughing, already busy with his catch. I soon called him over to help me corner a huge eel; we joined hands to catch it. Then came another; the mud spattered our faces; sometimes we would suddenly step into a hole and the water would rise to our thighs; we were soon soaked through. In the heat of the sport we exchanged no more than a few shouts, a few phrases; but at the day's end, I realized I was saying *"tu"* to Charles without quite knowing when I had begun. Working together had taught us more about each other than any long conversation. Marceline had not yet come, never did come, but already I no longer regretted her absence; it seemed to me she might have spoiled our fun a little.

The next day, I went back to the farm to look for Charles. We headed together for the woods.

Knowing so little about my own property and unconcerned to know more, I was amazed to learn that Charles knew not only the grounds but the various tenant farmers as well; I learned from him what I had barely suspected: I had six tenant farmers and might have realized sixteen to eighteen thousand francs a year in rents; if I made scarcely half that amount, it was because almost all the profits went into repairs and the payment of middlemen. The way Charles smiled when he glanced at the fields soon made me suspect that their yield was nowhere near so satisfactory as I had first supposed or as Bocage had led me to believe; I pressed Charles on this subject, delighted in the son by the purely practical intelligence which so exasperated me in the father. We continued our excursions day after day; the property was large, and when we had explored every corner of it, we started over again more methodically. Charles did not conceal his irritation at the sight of certain overgrown fields, stretches choked with bracken, thistles, sorrel; he managed to make me share his hatred for fallow land and to dream with him of a more highly organized kind of farming.

"But," I questioned him at first, "who suffers from the low yield? Only the tenant, isn't that right? No matter what he produces, the rent doesn't change."

Charles showed a touch of irritation. "You don't know what you're talking about," he ventured to answer—and I immediately smiled. "By considering only income, you don't realize your capital is deteriorating. Mistreating the soil makes it lose its value, little by little."

"If a tenant could produce more under a better system, I doubt if he'd refuse to try it—I know these people, they're too interested in profits not to make as much as they can."

"You're leaving out," Charles went on, "the increase in labor force. Some of these fields are far away from the farms. If they were cultivated, they'd bring in little or nothing, but at least they wouldn't go bad."

And the conversation continued. Sometimes, as we tramped the fields for an hour, we seemed to be repeating the same things over and over, but I listened and, little by little, I learned.

"After all, it's your father's business," I told him one day, losing patience.

Charles blushed. "My father's an old man," he said. "He's already got a lot to do making sure the leases are drawn up and the buildings repaired and the rents collected. It's not his job to make reforms here."

"What reforms would you propose?" I continued. But then he became evasive, claimed to have doubts; only by insisting could I force him to explain himself.

"Take away from the tenants every field they leave fallow," was his final advice. "If the farmers leave part of their land unfarmed, that just proves they don't need it all to pay you; or, if they try to keep it all, then raise the rents on their land. —They're all lazy around here," he added.

Of the six farms I found I owned, the one I preferred to visit was located on the hill overlooking La Morinière; it was called La Valterie, and its tenant was not a bad fellow; I enjoyed talking to him. Closer to La Morinière, a farm known as the "Château farm" was rented on a half-tenant system which left Bocage, in the landlord's absence, owner of some of the cattle. Now that my doubts were awakened, I began to suspect honest Bocage himself, if not of duping me at least of letting me be duped by others. A barn and a stable were reserved for me, it was true, but I soon realized they had been invented only so the tenant could feed his cows and horses on my hay and

oats. Till now I had listened indulgently to the most un-
likely stories Bocage told me from time to time: deaths,
malformations, diseases—I believed everything. It had
not yet occurred to me that as soon as one of the tenant's
cows fell sick it became mine, that as soon as one of my
cows was thriving it became the tenant's; however, a few
unguarded remarks from Charles, a few observations of
my own began to open my eyes; my mind, once alerted,
worked fast.

Marceline, at my request, carefully checked all the
accounts, but could discover no error in them; Bocage's
honesty took refuge there. —What was to be done?
—Leave well enough alone. —But at least, secretly irritated, I now supervised the stock, though without letting
it be too apparent.

I owned four horses and ten cows; enough to cause
me some apprehension. Of the four horses, one was still
called the "colt," though it was over three years old; it
was being broken in at the time; I had begun to take an
interest in it, when one day I was informed that the animal
was quite unruly, that nothing could be done with it, and
that I had best get rid of it. As if I had offered some
objection, the animal had been made to kick to pieces
the front of a small cart, bloodying its hocks in the
process.

I barely managed to keep my temper that day, and
what restrained me was Bocage's discomfort. After all,
the man is weak not wicked, I thought, the tenants are
to blame; but there's no authority for them to heed.

I went out into the farmyard to see the colt. As soon
as he heard me coming, a man who had been beating it
began to caress the animal. I acted as if I had seen
nothing. I knew little enough about horses, but this colt
looked like a fine one to me; it was a light-bay half-
breed with remarkably graceful lines; its eyes were very
bright, the mane and tail almost blond. I made certain
it was not hurt, ordered the scratches to be dressed and
left without another word.

That evening, when I saw Charles again, I tried to
find out what he thought of the colt.

"I think he's gentle enough," he told me; "but they don't know how to handle him; they'll turn him wild."

"How would you handle him?"

"If Monsieur would let me have him for eight days, I'll answer for that."

"What will you do?"

"You'll see."

The next day Charles took the colt out to a corner of the meadow under a splendid walnut tree in a curve of the river; I took Marceline along. It is one of the scenes I remember best. Charles had tied the colt by a rope several yards long to a stake pounded into the ground. Excessively nervous, the colt had apparently struggled for some time; exhausted now, it was circling the stake more calmly; its surprisingly elastic trot was agreeable to watch, as seductive as a dance. Charles stood in the center of the circle, avoiding the rope each time around with a sudden leap, and aroused or calmed the colt with his voice; he held a long whip in one hand, but I never saw him use it. Everything about his appearance and movements, his youth and his enjoyment, gave his task the fervent look of pleasure. All at once, I don't know how, he was riding the animal; it had slowed down, then stopped; Charles caressed it a moment, then suddenly I saw him astride it, sure of himself, scarcely holding onto its mane, laughing, bending over its neck, continuing to caress it. The colt had scarcely balked a moment; then it resumed its smooth trot, so handsome and supple that I envied Charles and told him so.

"Another few days' training and the saddle won't tickle him any more; in two weeks, Madame herself could mount him; he'll be gentle as a lamb."

He was telling the truth; a few days later, the horse let itself be caressed, saddled, led without mistrust; and even Marceline might have ridden it had her condition permitted such exercise.

"Monsieur should try him," Charles told me.

I would never have done this alone, but Charles offered to saddle another farm horse for himself; the pleasure of accompanying him won me over.

How grateful I was to my mother for sending me to

51

riding school when I was young! The distant memory of those first lessons came to my aid, and it did not seem so strange to be on horseback; in a few moments I felt no fear whatever and was quite at my ease. The horse Charles rode was heavier and not blooded at all, but handsome to look at; above all, Charles rode it well. We soon got into the habit of riding a little every day, preferring to start early in the morning through the grass still bright with dew; we reached the edge of the woods where the dripping hazels, shaken as we passed, soaked us through; suddenly the horizon opened; there was the broad Auge valley, and in the distance a suspicion of the sea. We stood for a moment, without dismounting; the dawning sun dyed, then dispersed, the mist; we returned at a brisk trot, lingering at the farm where work was just beginning; we savored that condescending pleasure of being ahead of the workers; then, as suddenly, we left them behind; I was back at La Morinière by the time Marceline was getting up. I returned drunk with air, dazed with speed, my limbs numb with a faint and voluptuous weariness, my spirits high, eager and fresh. Marceline approved, encouraged my whim. Still in boots, I brought to the bed where she lay expecting me a smell of wet leaves that she said she liked. And she listened to my accounts of our ride, the wakening of the fields, the work resuming. She seemed to take as much pleasure in hearing about my life as in living. —Soon I abused this pleasure too; our rides were extended, and sometimes I would not return until nearly noon.

Yet as often as I could I set aside the late afternoon and evening for the preparation of my lectures. I was pleased with my progress, and did not consider it out of the question that I might ultimately gather these lectures into a book. By a kind of natural reaction, even as my life was assuming an order and a shape, even as I delighted in ordering and shaping everything around me too, I grew increasingly enthusiastic about the crude morality of the Goths, and while throughout my lectures I insisted, with a boldness which was later a subject of some criticism, on exalting and even justifying savagery, I laboriously strove to master if not to suppress everything that might imply it around me and within me. To what lengths did I not carry this wisdom, or this folly?

Two of my tenants, eager to renew their leases, which would expire at Christmas, came to see me; they wanted me to sign the usual promissory lease. Bolstered by Charles's assurances, excited by his daily conversations, I waited for the tenants with my mind made up. They, convinced I would find it difficult to replace them, first demanded a rent reduction. Their amazement was all the greater when I read them the lease I had drawn up myself, in which I not only refused to lower the rent but even confiscated certain fields which I had seen they put to no use whatever. At first they pretended to take the matter lightly: I must be joking. What could I want with those fields? They were worthless; and if nothing had been done with them, it was because nothing could be done . . . Then, finding I was quite serious, they insisted; so did I. They tried to frighten me by threatening to leave. That was what I had been waiting for: "Well, leave then, if that's what you want! I'm not stopping you," I told them, tearing up the promissory leases before their eyes.

So I was left with over two hundred acres on my hands. For some time now I had planned to entrust their management to Bocage, supposing it was indirectly to Charles that I would be giving it; I also intended to deal with the land myself; as it was, I really gave very little thought to the matter: it was the risk of the venture which attracted me. The tenants would not be leaving until Christmas; until then we certainly had time to make up our minds. I informed Charles; his immediate delight irritated me; he could not conceal it, and I realized once again how much too young he was. Already time was of the essence: it was the season when the early harvests leave the fields free for the early plowing. Traditionally, the departing tenant's work is done alongside that of the incoming tenant, the former abandoning his holdings field by field as the harvest is brought in. I feared, as a kind of revenge, the animosity of the two tenants I had dismissed; on the contrary, they appeared to compy entirely with my demands (I learned only later the advantage this gave them). I profited by this opportunity to spend mornings and evenings on their fields, which were soon to revert to me. The autumn was beginning; I would have to hire more men in order to finish the plowing, the sowing; we had bought harrows, rollers, plows; I rode the colt over the land, supervising the work, enjoying my authority.

Meanwhile, in the neighboring fields, the apples were being harvested; they would fall, roll into the thick grass, abundant as never before; we did not have enough men to gather them; others came from the nearby villages, hired for eight days; Charles and I would occasionally entertain ourselves by helping them. Some of the men would beat the branches to bring down the late fruit; the apples that had fallen of themselves were harvested separately— overripe, often bruised, crushed in the high grass; you could not walk there without stepping on them. The odor rising from the meadow was pungent, sweetish, and mingled with the smell of the plowing.

The autumn was advancing. The mornings of the last fine days are the freshest, the clearest. Sometimes the moist air made the distances blue and even more remote, so that a ride became a journey; the country seemed larger; sometimes, on the other hand, the abnormal transparency of the air brought the horizon very close—a wingbeat away. I don't know which circumstance made me more listless. My work was nearly completed; at least I decided it was, in order to dare neglect it the more. The time I no longer spent at the farm I spent with Marceline. Together we would go out to the garden; we walked slowly, she trailing beside me, hanging on my arm; we would sit down on a bench overlooking the valley, which the evening filled with light. Marceline had a tender way of leaning against my shoulder; and we would stay there until dark, feeling the day dissolve in us, without movement, without speech.

Just as a breath of wind sometimes ripples smooth water, the slightest emotion could be read on Marceline's face; deep within herself she listened to the mysterious stirring of a new life; I bent over her as over a deep, clear pool which revealed, as far as one could see, nothing but love. Ah, if that was still happiness, I know I tried to hold onto it then, as one vainly tries to hold escaping water in one's cupped hands; yet already I sensed, close to our happiness, something besides happiness, which certainly stained my love, but as the autumn stains . . .

The autumn was advancing. The grass, wetter each morning, no longer dried under the branches at the edge of the woods; in the first light of day, it was white. The ducks splashed in the moat, fiercely beating their wings; sometimes they would all rise together, honking loudly, and circle the tower of La Morinière. One morning they vanished: Bocage had penned them up. Charles explained that they were shut away every autumn during the migrating season. And a few days later, the weather changed. Suddenly, one evening, a high wind blew in from the sea, strong and unwavering, bringing with it the north, the rain, sweeping away the migrant birds. Marceline's condition, the demands of moving, the first arrangements for my lectures, would have sent us to the city soon in any case. The bad weather, beginning early, drove us away.

Work on the farm, it is true, was to call me back in November. I had been very annoyed to learn of Bocage's winter plans; he announced his desire to send Charles back to the experimental farm where, Bocage claimed, he still had a great deal to learn; I talked to him for a long time, using every argument within reach, but failed to make him yield; at the very most he agreed to shorten these studies somewhat so that Charles could return a little sooner. Bocage made no secret of the fact that it would be difficult to manage the two newly vacated farms, but he had his eye, he informed me, on two very reliable farmers whom he intended to employ; the terms were too novel in this part of the country to augur much in their favor, but it was I, he kept saying, who had made the choice. —This conversation took place toward the end of October. In the first days of November, we returned to Paris.

We moved to the rue S——, near Passy. The apartment, which had been found for us by one of Marceline's brothers and which we had been able to inspect on our last trip through Paris, was much larger than the one my father had left me, and Marceline was rather worried not only by the higher rent but also by the many expenses such an establishment would involve. I countered all her fears with a factitious horror of anything temporary; I forced myself to believe in this reasoning, and exaggerated it on purpose. Certainly the cost of furnishing the new apartment would exceed our income for the year, but I counted on increasing our already considerable wealth by my lectures, by the publication of my book and even, how foolishly! by the new profits from my farms. I therefore spared no expense, telling myself each time that I was merely forming another tie to control any roving impulse I might feel, or feared to feel.

The first days, from morning to night, our time was spent shopping; and though Marceline's brother very obligingly volunteered later on to spare us some of the task, Marceline was soon feeling worn out. Then, instead of the rest she should have had once we were settled in, she was obliged to receive visit after visit; the out-of-the-way places we had lived hitherto made such calls all the more frequent now, and Marceline, unaccustomed to society, did not know how to shorten the visits and dared not close her door altogether; I would find her, by evening, utterly exhausted; and if I wasted no anxiety on a weariness whose cause I quite understood, at least I tried to diminish it by receiving in her stead, which I found rather tiresome, and sometimes by returning the calls myself, which I found altogether so.

I have never been a brilliant talker; the wit and frivolity of Parisian salons is something I could not enjoy; yet I had spent a good deal of time in some of them—but how long ago! What had happened since? With other people, I felt dull, sad, inept, both boring and bored. I was singularly unlucky in that none of you, whom I regarded as my only real friends, was in Paris; nor would you be returning for a long time. Could I have talked to you better? Would you have understood me better, perhaps, than I did myself? But what did I know of all that was growing within me, all that I am telling you today? The future looked quite certain, and never had I supposed myself more its master.

And even if I had been wiser, what recourse against myself could I have found in Hubert, Didier, Maurice, in so many others whom you know and judge as I do. I soon realized, unfortunately, the impossibility of making myself understood. From our very first conversations, I was more or less obliged by them to act a part—either to resemble the man they thought I still was, or else appear to be pretending; so to make things easier, I acted as if I had the thoughts and tastes they attributed to me. You cannot be sincere and at the same time seem so.

I was less reluctant to resume my professional connections, but in talking to archaeologists and philologists I had little more pleasure and no more emotion than in leafing through a good historical dictionary. At first I hoped to find a more direct understanding of life in the novelists and poets I knew—but if they possessed such a thing, they certainly kept it hidden; most of them, it seemed to me, did not live at all, were content with the appearance of life, and to them life itself seemed no more than a tiresome hindrance to writing. I could not blame them for this; nor do I assert that the mistake was not my own . . . Moreover, what did I mean by . . . living?

—That is precisely what I wanted them to tell me.

—The ones I met talked quite cleverly about life's various events, never about their causes.

As for the philosophers, whose role might have been to instruct me, I had long known what to expect of them; mathematicians or neo-Kantians, they kept as far as possible from troublesome reality, and were no more concerned with life than the algebrist with the existence of the quantities he is measuring.

Coming home to Marceline, I made no attempt to conceal the tedium of these encounters. "They're all alike," I told her, "and each repeats the next. Whenever I talk to one, it seems to me I'm talking to several."

"But my dear," Marceline answered, "you can't ask each one to be different from all the rest."

"The more they're like each other, the less they're like me." And I continued more wearily: "Not one of them has managed to be sick. They're alive, they seem to be alive and not to know it. As a matter of fact, since I've been with them, I've stopped being alive myself. Take today, for example. What did I do today? I must have left about nine this morning: there was scarcely time to do a little reading before then—the one good moment of the day. Your brother met me at the lawyer's, and after we left the office he went with me to the upholsterers; I had him on my hands at the cabinetmaker's too, and only got rid of him at Gaston's; I had lunch in the neighborhood with Philippe, then I met Louis, who had an appointment with me at a café; we went together to Théodore's ridiculous lecture, which I had to compliment him on when it was over; and to get out of his invitation for Sunday I had to go with him to Arthur's; Arthur took me to a watercolor show, and then I left cards at Albertine's and Julie's. I get home exhausted and find you just as tired as I am, after calls from Adeline, Marthe, Jeanne and Sophie. And now, tonight, when I review the whole day's occupations, I feel it's been so futile, so empty that I'd like to turn back the clock and start over again, hour by hour—and I'm so miserable I could cry."

Yet I couldn't have said what I meant by *living,* nor whether my longing for a more spacious and exposed life, a life less constrained and less concerned for others, was not the very secret of my uneasiness—a secret which seemed so much more mysterious: the secret of a Lazarus, for I was still a stranger among the others, like a man raised from the dead. At first I felt only a painful confusion; but soon a very different emotion appeared. I had taken no pride, I repeat, in the publication of the work which brought me so much praise. Was it pride I was feeling now? perhaps; but at least there was no trace of vanity in it. Actually, and for the first time, it was an awareness of my own worth: what separated me, what distinguished me from the rest was what mattered; what no one but I said or could say—that was what I had to say.

My lectures began soon afterward; on the strength of the subject, I charged that first hour with all my new passion. Discussing the decline of Latin civilization, I described artistic culture as rising like a secretion to the surface of a people, at first a symptom of plethora, the superabundance of health, then immediately hardening, calcifying, opposing any true contact of the mind with nature, concealing beneath the persistent appearance of life the diminution of life, forming a rind in which the hindered spirit languishes, withers and dies. Finally, carrying my notion to its conclusion, I said that Culture, born of life, ultimately kills life.

The historians found fault with what they called my tendency to generalize too readily. Others criticized my method; those who complimented me were those who had understood me least.

It was as I was leaving my lecture room that I saw Ménalque again for the first time. I had never seen much of him, and shortly before my marriage he had set off on another of those remote expeditions which kept him away for over a year at a time. In the past I had never liked him much; he seemed arrogant and took no interest in my life. I was therefore amazed to see him at my first lecture. His very insolence, which had first kept us apart, now pleased me, and I found his smile all the more charming because I knew it was not habitual. Lately an absurd, a shameful, lawsuit with scandalous repercussions had given the newspapers a convenient occasion to besmirch his name; those whom his scorn and superiority offended seized this opportunity for their revenge; and what irritated them most was that he seemed quite unaffected.

"You have to let other people be right," was his answer to their insults. "It consoles them for not being anything else."

But Society was outraged, and those who, as the saying goes, "respect themselves" felt obliged to cut him, thereby requiting his contempt. For me this was another inducement: drawn to him by a secret influence, I approached Ménalque and embraced him warmly in front of everyone.

Seeing with whom I was talking, the last bores withdrew; I remained alone with Ménalque. After the irritating criticisms and the inept compliments, his few words about my lecture were a relief. "You're burning what you once worshipped," he said. "Which is a good thing. You're catching fire late, but that means there's all the more to feed the flames with. I'm not yet sure I understand you completely; you interest me. It isn't easy for me to talk, but I'd like to talk to you. Have dinner with me tonight."

"Dear Ménalque," I answered, "you seem to forget I'm a married man."

"Yes, that's right," he continued. "The friendly way you came up to me just now made me forget you aren't free."

I was afraid of seeming weak even more than of having offended him, and I promised I would join him after dinner.

In Paris, where he was always *en passage*, Ménalque stayed at a hotel; for this visit he had had several rooms furnished as an apartment; his own servants waited on him, and he took his meals, like his life, alone; he had covered the walls and the furniture, whose commonplace ugliness offended him, with fabrics he had brought back from Nepal—he claimed he was adding a patina of dirt before giving them to some museum. I had been so eager to join him that I found him still at table when I went in, and apologized for interrupting his meal. "But I have no intention of interrupting it," he said. "I trust you'll allow me to finish. If you had come to dinner, I could have offered you Shiraz, the wine that Hafiz sang about, but now it's too late; you have to drink Shiraz on an empty stomach; at least you'll have some liqueurs, won't you?"

I accepted, assuming he would join me, and when only one glass was brought, I showed my surprise.

"Forgive me," he said, "I almost never drink them."

"Are you afraid of getting drunk?"

"Oh, quite the contrary! I happen to regard sobriety as a more powerful intoxication—in which I keep my lucidity."

"While you serve drinks to others?"

He smiled. "I can't ask everyone to reflect my virtues. It's enough to discover my vices in them."

"At least you smoke?"

"Just as rarely. Smoking's an impersonal, negative intoxication, and too easy to come by; I want an exaltation in my drunkenness, not a diminution of life. Let's not talk about that. Do you know where I've just been? Biskra! When I heard you had been there not long before, I tried to track you down. Why would he have come to Biskra, this blind scholar, this bookworm? As a rule I'm only discreet about the secrets people tell me; what I find out on my own is endlessly fascinating, I must admit. So I questioned, searched, nosed out whatever I could. My indiscretion served some purpose, since it made me want to see you again; and since instead of the routine pedant I used to see in you, I know I'm seeing now . . . you tell me what."

I felt myself blushing. "What did you find out about me, Ménalque?"

"Do you want to hear? Oh, don't worry—you know our friends well enough to know I can't talk about you to anyone. You saw how well they understood your lecture!"

"But I still don't see," I said rather testily, "why that means I can talk better to you than to the rest. Come on, what is it you found out about me?"

"First of all, you had been sick."

"But that has nothing to . . ."

"Oh, that's already very important. Then I was told you liked to go out alone, without a book (and that's when I began to wonder) or, when you weren't alone, accompanied by certain children in preference to your wife. Don't blush now, or I won't tell you the rest."

"Tell it without looking at me."

"One of the children—his name was Moktir, I believe—more attractive than most, more predatory than all of them—seemed to have a lot to say; I enticed him, Michel, I bought his confidence, which as you know isn't easy—I think he was lying even when he said he wasn't lying any more . . . You'll tell me if what he said about you is the truth." Meanwhile Ménalque had stood up and taken out of a drawer a tiny box which he opened. "Were these scissors yours?" he asked, handing me something shapeless, rusty, blunted, twisted; yet I had no difficulty recognizing the sewing scissors Moktir had filched from me.

"Yes; those are the ones—they belonged to my wife."

"He claims he took them from you while you weren't looking, one day when you were alone with him in your room; but that's not the interesting part; he also claims that at the very moment he hid them in his *burnous*, he realized you were spying on him in the mirror and caught the reflection of your eyes watching him. You saw the theft and said nothing! Moktir seemed very surprised by that silence . . . So was I."

"I'm just as surprised by what you're telling me now: you mean he knew I was watching him?"

"That's not the point; you were trying to outwit him; that's a game children always win. You thought you caught him and you were the one who got caught . . . That's not the point. What I want you to explain is your silence."

"I'd like an explanation myself."

Neither of us spoke for some time. Ménalque, who was walking up and down the room, absentmindedly lit a cigarette, then threw it away at once. "There is," he continued, "a 'sense,' the others would say, a 'sense' you seem to be lacking, my dear Michel."

"You mean a 'moral sense,' " I said, trying to smile.

"No, just a sense of property."

"You don't seem to have much of one yourself."

"I have so little that nothing you see here belongs to me; not even, or especially not, the bed I sleep on. I have a horror of comfort; possessions invite comfort, and in their security a man falls asleep; I love life enough to try to live wide awake, and so, even among all my treasures, I cherish a sense of the precarious, by which I provoke or at least arouse my life. I can't say I love danger, but I love a life of risk, I want life to demand of me, at every moment, all my courage, all my happiness, and all my health."

"Then why do you find fault with me?"

"My dear Michel, you don't understand me at all! And just when I was foolish enough to try making a profession of faith! . . . If I don't bother about other people's approval or disapproval, Michel, it's not to approve or disapprove in my turn; the words have no meaning for me. I was talking too much about myself just now; thinking you understood me carried me away . . . All I meant was that for a man without a sense of property you seem to own a great deal; that's a serious matter."

"What is the great deal that I own?"

"Nothing, if you take that tone about it . . . But aren't you beginning your lecture series? Don't you have an estate in Normandy? Didn't you just move into an apartment—and a luxurious one—in Passy? You're married. Aren't you expecting a child?"

"All of which," I said, provoked, "simply proves I've managed to make my life more 'dangerous,' as you would say, than yours."

"Yes, simply," Ménalque repeated ironically. Then turning suddenly and holding out his hand: "All right, goodbye; that's enough for tonight, and saying anything more won't help. But we'll see each other soon."

Some time passed before I saw him again.

New work, new worries preoccupied me; an Italian scholar sent me some unpublished documents he was editing, and I studied them exhaustively for my course. Realizing my first lecture had been misunderstood made me want to cast the rest in a different, more powerful form; thus I was led to offer as doctrine what I had first ventured as no more than an ingenious hypothesis. How many dogmatists owe their strength to the accident that their hints were not understood! In my own case, I confess I cannot tell how much stubbornness mingled with a natural need for assertion. The new things I had to say seemed the more urgent the more difficult it was for me to say them and, above all, to make them understood.

But how pale the phrases became, alas, in the face of action! Was not Ménalque's life, his slightest gesture, a thousand times more eloquent than my learning? How well I understood then that almost every ethical teaching of the great philosophers of antiquity was a teaching by example as much as—even more than—by words!

It was in my own home that I saw Ménalque again, nearly three weeks after our first meeting. It was toward the end of a large party. To avoid continual disturbance, Marceline and I preferred to hold an open house every Thursday evening—which made it easier to have a closed one the other days of the week. Every Thursday, then, the people who called themselves our friends would come; the spaciousness of our rooms made it possible to receive in great numbers, and the party often lasted very late. I think what attracted people most was Marceline's exquisite grace, and the pleasure of talking to each other. As for myself, after the second such evening, I had nothing more to say, nothing more to listen to, and found it difficult to conceal my boredom. I would wander from the den to the living room, from the library to the hall, sometimes detained by a phrase overheard, noticing little and glancing about almost at random.

Antoine, Étienne and Godefroy, sprawled in my wife's delicate armchairs, were discussing the latest vote in the Chambre des Députés. Hubert and Louis were carelessly handling and creasing some fine engravings from my father's collection. In the den, Mathias, in order to pay closer attention to Léonard, had set down his still-smoldering cigar on a rosewood tabletop. A glass of curaçao had spilled on the rug. Albert's muddy shoes, shamelessly resting on a couch, were staining the upholstery. And the dust we were all breathing was made up of the dreadful erosion of things . . . I was seized by a furious impulse to push all my guests out of the house. Furniture, fabrics, engravings, everything lost all its value for me at the first blemish—things stained, things infected by disease and somehow marked by mortality. I longed to protect everything, to put it all under lock and key for myself alone. How lucky Ménalque is, I thought, owning nothing! It's because I want to save things that I suffer. What does it all really matter?

In a small, softly lit salon entered through a glass door, Marceline received only her most intimate friends; she was propped up on some cushions, looking dreadfully pale and so exhausted that I was suddenly alarmed, and I resolved this would be our last party. It was already late. I was about to glance at my watch when I felt in my vest-pocket . . . Moktir's little scissors. Why had he stolen them, just to spoil them right away, to destroy them?

At that moment, someone tapped my shoulder; I whirled around—it was Ménalque. He was almost the only man there in evening dress. He had just arrived, and he asked me to introduce him to my wife; I certainly would not have done so of my own accord. Ménalque was elegant, almost handsome; an enormous drooping mustache, already gray, cut across his pirate's face; the cold fire of his gaze evinced more courage and will than kindness. He was no sooner standing in front of Marceline than I realized she didn't like him. After he had exchanged a few commonplaces with her, I led him into the den.

I had heard that very morning of his new assignment from the Colonial Ministry; several newspapers, reviewing his adventurous career in connection with it, seemed to forget their recent calumnies and could not find compliments enough to praise him. They vied with each other in exaggerating the services rendered to the nation, to all humanity, by the profitable discoveries of his latest expeditions, just as if he undertook nothing except with humanitarian intent; instances of his abnegation, dedication and intrepidity were extolled as if such praises should be regarded as a recompense.

I began to congratulate him, but he interrupted me at the first words: "What—you too, dear Michel? At least you didn't insult me first," he said. "Leave such nonsense to the newspapers. They seem amazed today that a man

65

of discredited tastes can still have any virtues at all. I cannot apply to myself the distinctions and the reservations they insist on making—I exist only as a whole man. I lay claim to nothing but my own nature, and the pleasure I take in an action is my clue to its propriety."

"That can take you far," I answered.

"I mean it to," Ménalque went on. "If only these people around us could be convinced. But most of them believe they get nothing good out of themselves except by constraint; they're only pleased with themselves when they're under duress. If there's one thing each of them claims not to resemble it's . . . himself. Instead he sets up a model, then imitates it; he doesn't even choose the model—he accepts it ready-made. Yet I'm sure there's something more to be read in a man. People dare not—they dare not turn the page. The laws of mimicry—I call them the laws of fear. People are afraid to find themselves alone, and don't find themselves at all. I hate all this moral agoraphobia—it's the worst kind of cowardice. You can't create something without being alone. But who's trying to create here? What seems different in yourself: that's the one rare thing you possess, the one thing which gives each of us his worth; and that's just what we try to suppress. We imitate. And we claim to love life."

I let Ménalque talk on; what he was saying was precisely what I had said to Marceline the month before, and I ought to have approved of it. Why, then, out of what cowardice, did I break in and repeat word for word the sentence with which Marceline had interrupted me then: "But my dear Ménalque, you can't ask each one to be different from all the rest."

Ménalque suddenly fell silent, stared at me strangely, and then, just when Eusèbe was coming up to say goodbye, turned his back quite rudely and began talking to Hector.

As soon as the words were out of my mouth, my remark seemed idiotic to me; and I particularly regretted it might make Ménalque think I felt threatened by his meaning. It was late; my guests were leaving. When the room was almost empty, Ménalque came up to me again: "I can't leave you this way," he said. "I probably misunderstood what you said. At least let me think I did."

"No," I answered. "You didn't misunderstand me. But what I said was meaningless, and as soon as I said it I began suffering from its stupidity, and especially from feeling it would make you identify me with the very people you were describing, the ones who are just as hateful to me—believe me—as they are to you. If there's one thing I detest it's a man of principles."

"You're right," Ménalque answered, laughing, "he's the most detestable kind of person in the world. You can't expect any kind of sincerity from him, for he only does what his principles have ordered him to do, or else he considers what he does as a transgression. The minute I suspected you might be such a man, I felt my words freeze on my lips. And my disappointment at that moment showed me how fond of you I was; I wanted to be wrong—not in my affection, but in my judgment of you."

"And it's true, your judgment wasn't the right one."

"No, it couldn't be," he said, suddenly seizing my hand. "Listen, I'm leaving Paris soon, but I'd like to see you again. This time my trip will be longer and more dangerous than the others; I don't know when I'll be coming back. I'm planning to start in two weeks; no one knows I'm leaving so soon—I'm telling you in confidence. I leave at dawn, and the night before such a departure is always one of terrible anxiety for me. Prove you're not a man of principles—can I count on you to spend that last night with me?"

"But we'll see each other again before that," I said, rather surprised.

"No. During these two weeks I won't even be in Paris. Tomorrow I leave for Budapest; in six days' time I have to be in Rome, and then Madrid: I want to embrace certain friends once more before leaving Europe."

"Of course, then, I'll keep that vigil with you."

"And we'll drink the wine of Shiraz," Ménalque said.

Several days after this evening, Marceline's health began to decline. I've already told you she was often tired; but she refused to complain, and because I attributed this

67

fatigue to her condition, I thought it quite natural and did not become concerned. Our old doctor—a fool or an ignoramus—had been overly reassuring from the first. New symptoms, however, accompanied by fever, convinced me to consult Dr. Tr——, then regarded as the leading specialist in the city. He was amazed I had not called him sooner, and prescribed a strict regimen Marceline should already have been following for some time. By foolhardy resolution, she had been overextending herself; from now on until the date of her confinement, around the end of January, she was to keep to her chaise longue. Probably alarmed and suffering more than she would admit, Marceline complied quite meekly with the most wearisome instructions; a kind of religious resignation broke the will which had sustained her till now, so that her condition grew suddenly worse during the next few days.

I nursed her with even more care, and reassured her as best I could, repeating the words of Dr. Tr—— himself, who saw nothing very serious in her condition; but the violence of her apprehensions ended by alarming me as well. How dangerously, already, our happiness rested on hope! and on a hope whose future was so uncertain! I, who originally had savored only the past, might at some point have been seduced by the sudden delights of the Moment, I reasoned—but the future dims the present even more than the present dimmed the past; ever since our night in Sorrento, all my love, all my life had been projected onto the future.

Meanwhile the evening came which I had promised to spend with Ménalque; and despite my reluctance to abandon Marceline for a whole winter's night, I did my best to convince her of the formality of the occasion, the seriousness of my promise. She was feeling a little better that evening, yet I was uneasy; a nurse took my place at her bedside. But once I was out in the street, my anxiety gained new strength; I scoffed at it, struggled against it, annoyed at being unable to free myself. Thus I worked myself into a state of extreme tension, of singular exaltation, at once very different from, yet very close to, the painful anxiety which had produced it, but even closer to happiness. It was late; I was walking fast, taking huge strides; snow was beginning to fall heavily; I was glad to breathe at last a keener air, to struggle with the cold; happy against the wind, the night, the snow; I savored my own energy.

Ménalque, who heard me coming, appeared on the landing. He had been waiting for me impatiently. He was pale, seemed rather tense. He helped me out of my coat, and made me change my wet boots for some soft Persian slippers. On a tray near the fire were set out some sweetmeats. Two lamps lit the room, though not so brightly as the fire on the hearth. Ménalque immediately asked after Marceline's health. To simplify matters, I answered that she was doing very nicely.

"And you're expecting your child soon?" he went on.

"In two months."

Ménalque leaned toward the fire as if to hide his face. He said nothing, and remained silent so long that I was finally embarrassed, uncertain what to say in my turn. I stood up, took a few steps, then went over to him and rested my hand on his shoulder. As if he were thinking aloud he murmured, "A man has to choose. What matters is to know what he wants."

"Do you mean you don't want to leave?" I asked him, uncertain of his meaning.

"So it seems."

"Why hesitate, then?"

"What's the use? You who have a wife and child—you stay. Of the thousand forms of life, each of us can know only one. Envying another man's happiness is madness: you wouldn't know what to do with it if you had it. Happiness isn't something that comes ready-made, to order. I'm leaving tomorrow; I know—I've tried to cut my happiness to my own measure. You keep your fireside happiness."

"I've cut my happiness to my measure too!" I exclaimed. "But I've grown. And now my happiness is too tight for me. Sometimes I'm almost strangled by it."

"Oh, you'll get used to it!" Ménalque said; then he turned and stood up in front of me, staring into my eyes, and when I found nothing to say, he smiled a little sadly:

"We imagine we possess, and we are possessed," he went on. "Pour yourself some Shiraz, dear Michel; you won't taste it often; and try some of those candied rose petals the Persians serve with it. This one night I want to drink with you, to forget I'm leaving tomorrow, to talk as if this night would last forever. Do you know why our poetry today and especially our philosophy are such dead issues? Because they've cut themselves off from life. Now, Greece idealized on life's own level: an artist's life was already a poetic achievement; a philosopher's life was an enactment of his philosophy; and when they were a part of life that way, instead of ignoring each other, philosophy could nourish poetry, poetry express philosophy, and together achieve an admirable persuasiveness. Today beauty no longer acts; and action no longer bothers about being beautiful; and wisdom operates on the sidelines."

"Why," I asked, "since you live your wisdom, why don't you write your memoirs?—or simply," I went on, seeing him smile, "what you remember of your travels?"

"Because I don't want to remember," he answered. "If I did, I might keep the future from happening by letting the past encroach upon it. I create each hour's newness by forgetting yesterday completely. *Having been* happy is never enough for me. I don't believe in dead things. What's the difference between no longer being and never having been?"

I was angered, finally, by these remarks which were too far ahead of my own thoughts; I wanted to draw back, to stop him, but could not find a way to contradict his words, and besides I was even more annoyed with myself than with Ménalque. So I said nothing. He, pacing back and forth like a caged animal, then bending over the fire, kept silent a long while, then blurted out, "If only our wretched brains could really embalm our memories! But memories don't keep well. The delicate ones wither, the voluptuous ones rot, the most delicious ones are the most dangerous later on. The things you repent were delicious once . . ."

Another long silence, and then he went on: "Regret, remorse, repentance—they're all former joys, reversed. I don't like looking back, and I leave my past behind me the way a bird leaves its shady tree in order to fly away. I tell you, Michel, each joy still awaits us, but must find the bed empty, must be the *only one,* so that we come to it like a widower. Oh Michel, each joy is like manna in the desert, which spoils from one day to the next; or like water from the fountain of Ameles which Plato says no pitcher could preserve. Let each moment carry away whatever it has brought."

Ménalque talked on much longer; I cannot repeat here everything he said; yet many of his phrases were etched into my mind, the more deeply because I wanted to forget them; not that they told me much that was new, but they suddenly laid bare my own mind: thoughts I had covered with so many veils I almost believed they were smothered. And so the vigil passed.

When, in the morning, after accompanying Ménalque to the train that took him away, I walked home alone to rejoin Marceline, I was filled with a hideous melancholy, with hatred of Ménalque's cynical joy; I wanted it to be false—I tried to deny it. I grew angry at having been unable to answer him; angry at having spoken words that made him doubt my love, my happiness. And I clung to my doubtful happiness, my "fireside happiness" as he called it; I could not protect it from my anxiety, but I told myself that anxiety was the food of love. I yearned toward the future where already I saw my new baby smiling at me; because of that child my spirits were strengthened, renewed. Already I was walking with a firm step.

But when I returned that morning, an unaccustomed disorder alarmed me as soon as I went in. The nurse met me and in carefully chosen words reported that my wife had suffered painful spasms during the night, though she did not think she had begun labor yet; feeling very ill, she had sent for the doctor, and the latter, though he had come at once in the middle of the night, had not yet left his patient; then, seeing me turn pale, I suppose, she tried to reassure me, telling me that everything was much better now, that ... I rushed to Marceline's room.

The room was dimly lit, and at first I could make out only the doctor, whose hand was held up for silence; then,

71

in the shadows, a figure I did not recognize. Anxiously, without a sound, I approached the bed. Marceline's eyes were closed; she was so terribly pale that at first I thought she was dead; but without opening her eyes she turned her head toward me. In a dark corner of the room, the unknown figure was putting away or hiding various objects; I glimpsed shiny instruments, surgical cotton; I saw or thought I saw a bloodstained sheet . . . I felt faint and almost fell into the doctor's arms; he supported me. I understood; I was afraid of understanding.

"The baby?" I asked anxiously.

He shrugged sadly. —Without realizing what I was doing, I flung myself against the bed, sobbing. Ah, the sudden future! The ground had given way under my feet; before me was nothing but an empty hole into which I stumbled headlong.

Here everything dissolves in shadowy recollections. Yet Marceline seemed at first to recover quite rapidly. The New Year's vacation allowed me some respite, and I could spend almost every hour of the day at her side, where I read, wrote or read aloud to her quietly. I never left the house without bringing her flowers when I returned. I recalled the tender care she had lavished on me when I had been ill, and surrounded her with so much love that sometimes she smiled at me as if she were happy. Not a word was spoken about the sad accident which had destroyed our hopes.

Then phlebitis set in; and when that began to subside, an embolism suddenly kept Marceline between life and death. It happened at night; I can still see myself leaning over her, feeling my own heart stopping and starting with hers. How many nights of vigil I spent there! my eyes stubbornly fixed upon her, hoping by the strength of love to insinuate a little of my own life into hers. And if I no longer thought much about happiness, my one sad satisfaction was to see Marceline smile occasionally.

My lectures had begun again. Where did I find the strength to prepare them, to deliver them? My memory is vague, and I don't know how the weeks went by. Yet I want to tell you one little incident:

It happened one morning, soon after the embolism; I

am sitting with Marceline, who seems to be feeling a little better, but strict immobility is still prescribed; she cannot even raise her arms. I bend down to give her something to drink, and when she is through and I am still leaning over her, in a voice her emotion makes still weaker she asks me to open a box she indicates with her eyes alone; it is over there, on the table; I open it; it is full of ribbons, bits of cloth, worthless ornaments. What does she want? I bring it to the bed and take out each object one by one. Is it this? this? . . . No; not yet; and I sense she's growing a trifle uneasy. "Oh, Marceline, is it this little rosary you want?" She tries to smile. "Are you afraid I'm not taking enough care of you?"

"Oh my dear!" she murmurs. —And I remember our conversation in Biskra, her timid reproach when I rejected what she called "God's help."

I continue a little harshly: "I did manage to get well by myself."

"I prayed for you so much," she answers. She says this tenderly, mournfully; I recognize an imploring anxiety in her eyes. I take the rosary and slip it into the weakened hand lying on the sheet at her side. A loving, tearful glance rewards me, but I cannot respond; I linger another moment, not knowing what to do, embarrassed; finally, unable to bear any more, I say, "Goodbye for now," and leave the room, hostile, as if I had been driven out.

Meanwhile the embolism had been followed by serious complications; the dreadful blood clot, which the heart had rejected, exhausted and congested her lungs, obstructed her breathing, which was now labored and wheezing. Sickness had entered Marceline, henceforth inhabited her, marked her, soiled her. She was a tainted thing.

III

The weather was turning mild. Once my lectures were over I moved Marceline to La Morinière, the doctor assuring me that all immediate danger was past and that, to complete her recovery, nothing was more necessary than better air. I myself needed rest badly. The virtually unassisted night watches I had insisted on keeping, the prolonged anxiety, and above all the kind of physical sympathy which, at the time of Marceline's embolism, had reproduced the dreadful spasms of her heart in mine—all this had exhausted me as if I myself had been sick.

I should have preferred taking Marceline to the mountains; but she pleaded to return to Normandy, insisted that no climate could be better for her, and reminded me of the two farms I had rather recklessly undertaken to manage. She convinced me that I had assumed responsibility for them, that I owed it to myself to make them succeed. The moment we arrived, she urged me to have a look at the fields . . . I suspect there was a good deal of abnegation in her friendly prodding; fear that I might feel tied to her by the care she still required, and not free enough . . . Yet Marceline was recovering; blood had brought fresh color to her cheeks, and nothing reassured me more than to see her smile less wanly; I could leave her without apprehension.

I therefore returned to the farms. The first hay was being cut. The air heavy with pollen, with perfume, went to my head at once like some powerful drink. I felt I had not breathed for a year, or had breathed only dust, so gently did the atmosphere enter my lungs. From the slope where I was sitting, half intoxicated, I overlooked La Morinière; I saw its blue roofs, the sleeping waters of its moat; around it, mown fields and others where the grass was still high; beyond them the curve of the stream; farther still, the woods where I had gone riding the preceding autumn with Charles. The sound of singing I had been hearing for several minutes grew nearer; it was the haymakers coming home, rakes or pitchforks on their shoulders. These workmen, almost all of whom I recognized, reminded me with a start that I was not here as a delighted tourist, but as their employer. I went up to them, smiling and asking after each man at length. That very morning Bocage had managed to inform me as to the state of the crops; moreover his frequent letters had kept me informed about even the most trivial matters at the farms. The prospect was not so bad—much better than Bocage had at first led me to expect. Yet a number of important decisions depended on my presence, and for several days I managed everything to the best of my ability, taking no pleasure in the task but propping, on this semblance of work, my disheveled life.

Once Marceline was well enough to receive visitors, some friends came to stay with us. Their affectionate, staid society appealed to Marceline, but sent me out of the house all the more readily. I preferred the company of the farm people; it seemed to me that I had more to learn from them—not that I asked them so many questions; no; indeed I can scarcely express the kind of pleasure I took in being with them: it was as if I could feel *through* them; and while the conversation of our friends was already entirely familiar before they opened their mouths, the mere sight of these laborers caused me a continual amazement.

If at first they seemed to answer my questions with all the condescension I had avoided in putting them, they soon grew more tolerant of my presence. I felt I was coming closer to them. Not content to oversee their work, I wanted to watch them at play; their clumsy thoughts were of no interest to me, but I shared their meals, I listened to their jokes, lovingly observed their pleasures. It was the same kind of sympathy that had made my heart respond to Marceline's spasms, an immediate echo of each alien sensation, not vague in the least but exact, acute. I felt in my own arms the stiffness of the mower's; I was weak with his weariness; the mouthful of cider he drank slaked my thirst; I felt it slide down his throat; one day, sharpening his scythe, a man cut his thumb deeply: I felt the pain of it, to the bone.

And I seemed to be learning about the land with more than my eyes alone—I *felt* it now, by some sense of touch to which this strange sympathy of mine set no limits.

Bocage's presence embarrassed me: when he came I had to play the landowner, a role I no longer enjoyed. I still gave what orders were necessary and directed the men in my own way, but I no longer rode through the fields on horseback lest I seem to be looking down on them. Yet despite all my precautions to keep them from feeling constrained by my presence, I remained with them, as before, perversely inquisitive. Each of their lives held a mystery—it still seemed to me that something was hidden. What did they do when I was no longer there? I refused to believe they had nothing better to do, and I ascribed to each a man a secret I was determined to learn. I lurked, prowled, stalked. I deliberately attached myself to the crudest natures, as if out of such darkness I expected to be shown the way by a sudden light.

One man in particular attracted me: tall, rather handsome, not stupid but guided solely by instinct; he did nothing save on the spur of the moment, yielded to every passing impulse. He was not from this part of the country, but had been hired for the time being. An excellent worker for two days, he would be dead drunk the third. One night I crept down to the barn to have a look at him; he lay sprawling in the hay; his sleep was the heavy trance of intoxication. How long I stared at him! . . . Then one day he vanished as he had come. By what roads, I wondered. That same evening I heard that Bocage had fired him. I sent for Bocage in a rage.

"I hear you've fired Pierre," I began. "Can you tell me why?"

Somehow startled by my anger, which I was nonetheless doing my best to control, he answered: "But Monsieur wouldn't want to keep a dirty drunk like that on the place—he was spoiling all the best workmen."

"I know which men I want to keep here better than you do."

"A tramp! No one even knows where he comes from. It gave the place a bad name. How would Monsieur like it if he set the barn on fire some night?"

"That's my business, and it's my farm as well. I mean to run it the way I choose. In the future, be sure you give me your reasons before you send anyone away."

Bocage, I have said, had known me as a child; however sharp the tone of my words, he was too fond of me to be really annoyed. And in fact he did not take me seriously enough. The Normandy peasant too often remains unconcerned by actions whose motives he cannot understand—that is, actions not prompted by the hope of profit. Bocage regarded this argument as no more than a whim of mine.

I had no desire, though, to end the discussion with a reproach, and feeling that I had been too hard on him, I tried to find something else to say. "Your son Charles will be coming home soon, won't he?" I managed to ask, after a moment's silence.

"I thought Monsieur had forgotten all about him," Bocage replied, still wounded.

"Forget him, Bocage! How could I forget him, after all the things we did together last year? As a matter of fact, I'm counting on him to help me with the farms."

"Monsieur is very kind. Charles will be home in a week's time."

"Well, I'm glad to hear it, Bocage." And I sent him off.

Bocage came close to the truth: I had not forgotten Charles, of course, but my interest in him was very slight. How can I explain that after so intense a friendship I no longer felt more than a peevish curiosity about him? The answer is that my tastes were no longer those of the year before. My two farms, I had to admit to myself, no longer interested me so much as the workmen I employed on them; and if I was to spend my time among these people, Charles's presence would be a hindrance. He was much too reasonable, much too respectable. So in spite of the deep feeling I attached to his memory, I rather dreaded his return.

He returned. How right I had been to dread, and how right Ménalque was to reject all memories! Instead of Charles, into the room walked a ridiculous Monsieur under an even more ridiculous bowler. Lord, how he had changed! Embarrassed, uneasy, I nonetheless tried not to spoil his evident pleasure in seeing me again; but even his pleasure vexed me by its clumsiness and what I took to be a certain insincerity. I had received him in the salon, and at that hour of the afternoon I couldn't see his face clearly; but when the lamps were brought in I noticed with disgust that he had let his whiskers grow.

Our conversation that evening was rather dull; for about eight days afterward, as I knew he would be at the farms continually, I avoided them and confined myself to my desk and to the company of my guests. Then, as soon as I began going out again, I was absorbed by an altogether new occupation.

Woodcutters had invaded the woods. Every year, some of the timber on the estate was sold; divided into twelve equal lots, the woods annually furnished, along with some full-size trees, the twelve-year growth that was cut up for faggots.

This work was done in winter and then, according to the terms of their contract, the woodcutters were to have cleared the lot before spring. But the negligence of old Heurtevent, the contractor, was so great that sometimes spring came and the lot was still covered with fallen trees; then the delicate new shoots had to creep through the dead branches, and when the woodcutters finally cleared the ground, many of the saplings were destroyed.

That year old Heurtevent's laxness was worse than we had feared. In the absence of any competing bids, I had had to lease the lot to him at a very low price; and so, certain of his profit, he was very slow about clearing what had cost him so little. From week to week he postponed the job, offering one excuse after another—the lack of workmen, the bad weather, a sick horse, other commitments . . . The consequence was that by midsummer, nothing had been cleared away.

What would have enraged me the year before left me quite calm now; I certainly saw the damage Heurtevent was causing, but the devastated woods were beautiful, and I wandered through them with delight, spying on the game I found there, startling the vipers and sometimes sitting for a long time on one of the fallen trunks that seemed still alive and was sending out a few green sprigs from its wounds.

Then, suddenly, in the second week of August, Heurtevent decided to send his men. Six came at once, claiming they would finish the whole job in ten days. The lot to be cleared was almost adjacent to La Valterie; to speed their work, I arranged to have the men's meals brought from the farm. The man given this job was a yokel named Bute, who had returned a complete wreck from his military service—I refer to his mind, for his body was in magnificent condition; he was one of my farmhands with whom I most enjoyed talking. And now I could see more of him without visiting the farm. For it was precisely at this time that I began going out again. And for several days I scarcely left the woods, returning to La Morinière only for meals, and often late for them. I pretended to be overseeing the work, but in truth saw only the workmen.

Sometimes two of Heurtevent's sons joined this crew of six men: one about twenty, the other fifteen, both lanky, bowlegged, hard-featured boys. They had a foreign look, and I learned later on that their mother was Spanish. I was surprised at first that she could have come such a distance, but Heurtevent, a rolling stone in his youth, had apparently married her in Spain. For this reason he was regarded disapprovingly in the neighborhood. The first time I noticed the younger boy, I remember, was a rainy day; he was alone, perched on a cartload of faggots, lying back among the branches and singing, or rather bawling, a strange kind of chant I had never heard in this region. The cart horses knew the road and followed it without any guidance. I cannot describe the effect that song produced on me, for I had heard its like only in Africa. The boy seemed to be in a trance, and might have been drunk; when I passed, he didn't even glance at me. The next day I found out this was Heurtevent's son. It was in order to see him again, or at least in the hope of seeing him, that I lingered in the woods now. They were soon cleared. The Heurtevent boys came only three times. They seemed proud, and I could not get a word out of them.

Bute, on the contrary, enjoyed talking; I managed to make it clear that he could say whatever he pleased, at which point he lost no time undressing the region. Greedily I brooded over the mystery. At one and the same time it exceeded my hopes and failed to satisfy me. Was *this* what simmered beneath appearances? or was it perhaps only one more hypocrisy, one more deception?

What if it was! And I questioned Bute as I had questioned the shapeless chronicles of the Goths. His stories gave off a murky vapor, a touch of brimstone which was already going to my head and which I uneasily inhaled. From him I learned first of all that Heurtevent was sleeping with his daughter. I was afraid of stopping the flow of confidences by giving the slightest sign of disapproval, so I merely smiled, curiosity urging me on. "And the mother? Doesn't she have anything to say about it?"

"The mother! She's been dead twelve years now . . . He used to beat her."

"How many are there in the family?"

"Five children. You saw the oldest son and the youngest. There's another about sixteen, a weakling who wants to be a priest. The older daughter already has two children by her father . . ."

And little by little I learned many other things which made the house of Heurtevent into a lurid, sulfurous place around which my helpless imagination circled like a blowfly: one night, the older son tried to rape a young servant girl, and when she put up a struggle the father intervened in his son's behalf, holding her down with his enormous hands; meanwhile the second boy, on the floor above, continued tenderly reciting his prayers and the youngest, a witness to the drama, enjoyed it all. As for the rape, I suppose it hadn't been very difficult, for Bute also told me that soon afterward the girl, having taken a liking to such things, had tried to seduce the little priest.

"And hasn't succeeded?" I asked.

"He's still holding out, but it won't be long now," Bute answered.

"Didn't you say there was another daughter?"

". . . who takes whatever she can get; and for nothing. When she really wants it, she's willing to pay. Except you can't do it in the house—the father would beat your head in. He says people can do what they want under their own roof—but not outsiders. Pierre—that farmhand you fired—didn't talk about it much, but one night he only got out of there with a dent in his head. And since then you do it in the woods."

"Have you had a try?" I asked, with an encouraging glance.

He lowered his eyes for form's sake and said, sniggering: "Once in a while." Then, suddenly looking up: "Old Bocage's boy too."

"What boy is that?"

"Alcide, the one who sleeps at the farm. Monsieur doesn't know who I mean?"

I was utterly amazed to learn that Bocage had another son.

"That's right," Bute went on. "Last year he was still at his uncle's. But it's odd that Monsieur hasn't met him yet in the woods. He goes out poaching almost every night."

Bute had said these last words in a lower voice. He stared at me, and I realized I had to smile. Satisfied, he went on: "Monsieur knows perfectly well what's going on. Anyway the woods are so big it doesn't do much harm."

I showed so little annoyance that soon after this, Bute, reassured and eager, I suppose, to settle some old scores with Bocage, showed me, in a certain glade, the snares set by Alcide and then took me to a place where I was almost sure to catch him. At the top of a rise in the thicket that formed the edge of the woods, there was a gap through which Alcide was in the habit of slipping at around six o'clock. Here Bute and I, delighted by our stratagem, stretched a copper wire, perfectly concealed. Then, having made me swear not to give him away, Bute went off, not wanting to compromise himself. I lay down on the slope; I waited.

And for three nights I waited in vain. I was beginning to think Bute had tricked me. The fourth evening, at last, I heard light footsteps approaching. My heart began pounding, and at that moment I learned the poacher's voluptuous dread. The snare was so well set that Alcide walked right into it. I saw him suddenly pitch forward, his ankle caught. He tried to get up but fell again, struggling like a trapped animal. But I had hold of him by then. He was a nasty-looking boy, green-eyed, towheaded, weasel-faced. He gave me a couple of kicks and then, immobilized, tried to bite my hands; when that proved futile he began pouring out a stream of the most extraordinary abuse I had ever heard. In the end I could stand it no longer and burst out laughing. At that he suddenly stopped, peered up at me and said, in a lower voice, "You brute, you've crippled me!"

"Let's have a look."

He pulled his sock down over his boot and showed his ankle, on which I could barely make out a faint pinkish line. "That's nothing."

He smiled a little, and then, slyly: "I'll tell my father you're the one who sets the snares."

"But it's one of your own!"

"I don't mean *you* set this one."

"How do you know?"

"You couldn't do it that well. Let me see how you do it."

"You teach me."

That evening I came in very late for dinner, and because no one knew where I had been, Marceline was distressed. But I didn't tell her I had set six snares, and that far from scolding Alcide I had given him ten sous.

The next day, making the rounds with him, I had the diversion of finding two rabbits caught in our snares; naturally I let him have them. The hunting season hadn't yet begun—what would he do with this game, which couldn't be sold publicly without getting him into trouble? Alcide refused to tell me. Finally I learned, from Bute again, that Heurtevent was the receiver and his youngest son the go-between. Was this the means by which I could learn more about this savage family? With what passion I continued poaching!

I met Alcide every evening; we caught a great many rabbits and even, once, a roebuck that still showed some faint signs of life. I'm still horrified when I remember Alcide's delight in killing it. We put the carcass in a safe place where the Heurtevent boy could come and find it during the night.

From then on I no longer cared much for going out by day, when the cleared woods attracted me so much less. I even tried to work; a pathetic, purposeless work—for when my lectures had ended I had refused to renew my appointment—thankless work from which I was abruptly distracted by the slightest song, the slightest sound in the countryside; every cry became for me a summons. How many times I jumped up from my desk to the window, to see nothing at all! How many times I dashed outside . . . The only attention of which I was capable was that of my five senses.

But once night fell—and night, even at this season, fell quickly—that was our time, whose beauty I had never suspected until then; and I stole out of the house the way thieves steal in. I had developed the eyesight of a night bird; I marveled at the richer, higher grass, the thicker foliage. Night magnified everything, opened everything, made the earth distant and every surface deep. The smoothest path seemed dangerous. Everywhere I sensed awakening whatever lived a life of darkness.

"Where does your father think you are right now?"

"Minding the cows, in the stable."

I knew that Alcide slept there, up near the pigeons and the hens; locked in at night, he managed to escape through a hole in the roof; his clothes retained the warm smell of fowls.

Then quite suddenly, as soon as the game was collected, he vanished into the night as though through a trapdoor, without a gesture, without even mentioning the next night's meeting. I knew that before returning to the farm, where the dogs never barked at him, he would find young Heurtevent and give him his catch. But where? I never managed to find out: bribes, threats, tricks, all failed; the Heurtevents wouldn't let anyone near them. And I don't know which was the greater triumph of my madness: to pursue a stupid mystery which forever receded before me, or perhaps to invent the mystery out of my own curiosity. —But what was it Alcide did when he left me? Did he actually sleep at the farm? Or only allow the farmer to think so? No matter how I compromised myself, I succeeded only in lessening his respect without increasing his confidence; which infuriated and at the same time depressed me.

Once he had vanished, I felt terribly alone, and

tramped home through the dew-soaked fields drunk on darkness and the wild, anarchic life around me, drenched, muddy, covered with leaves. From far away, in the sleeping house, I seemed to be guided, as though by a calm beacon, by the lamp in my study where Marceline supposed I was working away, or by the night light in Marceline's bedroom. I had persuaded her that without these nocturnal expeditions I could not fall asleep. It was the truth: I despised my bed, and would have preferred the barn.

Game was abundant that year. Rabbits, hares, pheasants filled the snares. After three nights, seeing that everything was going well, Bute decided to join us.

On our sixth night of poaching we found only two of our twelve traps: a raid had been made during the day. Bute asked me for a hundred sous to buy copper wire, the ordinary kind being useless.

The next day I had the pleasure of seeing my ten snares in Bocage's house, and I was even obliged to approve his zeal. The worst of it was that the year before, I had recklessly promised ten sous for each snare discovered: I now had to give Bocage a hundred. Meanwhile, with *his* hundred sous Bute bought more copper wire. Four days later, the same events; ten new traps were expropriated. Again, a hundred sous to Bute, and a hundred to Bocage. And when I congratulated him he answered, "It's not me you should thank, Monsieur, it's Alcide."

"Oh . . ." But too much astonishment might ruin everything. I controlled myself.

"Yes," Bocage went on, "Monsieur understands. I'm not a young man any more, and the farm takes up too much of my time. The boy keeps an eye on the woods for me; he knows them like the back of his hand—he's sharp, that boy of mine, he knows just where to look for the traps, and he finds them too."

"I can believe that, Bocage."

"So out of the ten sous Monsieur gives me, I let him have five on each trap."

"He certainly deserves it. Imagine, twenty snares in

five days! He does his job well. The poachers had better watch out—I suppose they'll lie low now."

"Oh no, Monsieur, the more you pick up, the more you find. Game is bringing a good price this year, and for the few sous it costs them . . ."

I had been so thoroughly taken that I almost thought Bocage was part of the ring. And what infuriated me about the business was not so much Alcide's triple-dealing as seeing him fool me this way. Besides, what were he and Bute doing with the money? I didn't have a clue—I would never know anything about such creatures. They would always lie, would cheat me for the sake of cheating me. That night it wasn't a hundred sous but ten francs I gave to Bute: I warned him that they were the last, and that if the traps were stolen again, it would be just too bad.

The next day, Bocage came to see me; he appeared very embarrassed; I immediately became more so. What had happened? Bocage informed me that Bute had not come back to the farm until after daybreak—and dead drunk; at Bocage's first words Bute had insulted him in filthy language, and then had attacked and beaten him.

"So I came to find out," Bocage said, "if Monsieur will authorize me" (and he lingered slightly on the word), "authorize me to fire him."

"Let me think it over, Bocage. I'm very sorry to hear he was disrespectful to you. I understand. Come back in two hours. I'll decide by then."

Bocage left.

To keep Bute was painfully unfair to Bocage; to dismiss him was to risk his revenge. Well, whatever came of it, I was the only guilty party. And as soon as Bocage returned I told him: "You can tell Bute we don't want to see him around here any more."

Then I waited. What was Bocage doing? What was Bute saying? —And only that evening did I hear rumors of the scandal. Bute had talked. I first realized this by the screams coming from Bocage's house—it was young Alcide being beaten. Bocage would be coming; he came—I heard his old footsteps, and my heart pounded even harder than when I had been poaching. An unbearable moment! A lot of fine feelings would have to be trotted out, and I would be obliged to take Bocage seriously. What explanations could I invent? How badly I would do it all! If only I could have given up my part . . . Bocage came in. I didn't understand a word of what he was saying. It was ridiculous: I had to make him start all over. Finally I managed to make out this much: He believed that Bute alone was guilty. The incredible truth escaped him: that I had given Bute ten francs—for what? He was too much of a Normandy peasant to conceive of such a thing. Bute must have stolen the ten francs, that was all; by claiming I had given them to him, he was merely proving himself a liar as well as a thief; it was a way of covering up, and Bocage wasn't the man to believe such a story. There was no more mention of poaching. If Bocage had beaten Alcide, it was because the boy had spent the night out.

So I was saved! In Bocage's eyes, at least, everything was all right. What a fool Bute was! That evening, I must admit, I didn't have much of a desire to go out poaching.

I had supposed then that everything was over, but an hour later Charles appeared. He looked anything but friendly—as he came toward me it occurred to me that he was even more of a bore than his father. To think that just a year before . . .

"Well, Charles, it's been a long time since I've seen you."

"If Monsieur wanted to see me, I was down at the farm. All you had to do was come there—but I don't spend my time in the woods at night."

"Ah, your father told you . . ."

"My father told me nothing because my father knows nothing. Why should he have to learn, at his age, that Monsieur is making a fool of him?"

"Watch out, Charles, don't say something you'll be sorry for."

"Oh, you're the master here, all right. You do whatever you please."

"Charles, you know perfectly well I've never made a

fool of anyone, and if I do what I please, it harms no one but myself."

He shrugged slightly. "How can you expect us to protect your interests if you undermine them yourself? You can't defend both the poacher and the gamekeeper."

"Why not?"

"Because then . . . Oh, listen, Monsieur, you're all too smart for me. I just don't like to see my employer siding with criminals and helping them undo the work we've done for him."

Charles's voice grew more and more assured. He sounded almost noble. I noticed that he had shaved off his whiskers. His point, moreover, was quite well taken. And since I said nothing (what could I have said?) he went on: "It was Monsieur who taught me last year that property involves certain responsibilities—but Monsieur seems to have forgotten. Either you take those responsibilities seriously and stop dealing with those . . . or else you don't deserve to own anything."

A silence.

"Is that all you came to say?"

"For tonight, yes, Monsieur. But some other night, if Monsieur forces me, perhaps I'll be coming to tell you that my father and I are leaving La Morinière." And he went out, after a very low bow. I took no time to reflect:

"Charles!" He's absolutely right . . . Oh, but if that's what's called ownership! . . . "Charles!" . . . And I ran after him, catching up with him in the dark, speaking very quickly, as though to bolster my sudden decision: "You can tell your father I'm putting La Morinière up for sale."

Charles bowed gravely and walked away without a word.

All of which was ridiculous, ridiculous!

That evening Marceline could not come down to dinner, and sent word that she was ill. I rushed upstairs and into her bedroom, full of anxiety. She reassured me at once: "It's only a cold." She had caught a chill, nothing more: "Though I put on my shawl the minute I started shivering."

"You should have put on something warmer."

"I should have put it on before I started shivering, not after." She looked at me, tried to smile. Perhaps a day that had begun so badly inclined me to anxiety. If she had actually spoken the words: "Do you really care so much whether I live or die?" I couldn't have understood her more clearly. No doubt about it, everything was going to pieces around me; of all that my hand grasped, it could hold onto nothing. I flung myself upon Marceline and covered her pale forehead with kisses. That was when she broke down and began sobbing on my shoulder.

"Oh, Marceline, Marceline! Let's get away from this place. Somewhere else I'll love you the way I did in Sorrento. You thought I had changed, didn't you? But somewhere else, you'll see, nothing has changed our love."

I had not yet cured her unhappiness, but already, how she clung to hope!

The summer was barely over, but already the weather was damp and cold; the last rosebuds were rotting unopened on the bushes. Our guests had long since left us. Marceline was so ill that she could not deal with closing the house, and five days later we left.

PART THREE

*T*hus I tried, and once again, to close my hand over my love. But what need had I of calm happiness? What Marceline gave me and what she meant to me was like rest to a man who is not tired. Yet I realized how exhausted *she* was, how much she needed my love, and I enveloped her within it, pretending that the need was mine. I felt her suffering unbearably; it was to heal her that I loved her.

Ah, that devoted care, those tender vigils! As other men goad their faith by exaggerating its observances, so I fostered my love. And Marceline, I tell you, took hope once more. In her there was still so much youth; in me, so much promise—she believed. We fled Paris as though embarking on another honeymoon. But even the first day of the journey she began to feel much worse; when we reached Neuchâtel we had to stop.

How I loved that lake whose yellowish banks had nothing Alpine about them, and whose marshlike waters slowly worked into the earth, filtering between the reeds. I was able to find a room for Marceline in a very comfortable hotel overlooking this lake; I did not leave her all day long.

She was so ill that the next day I sent for a doctor from Lausanne. He was concerned, quite uselessly, to know whether I had already heard of other cases of tuberculosis in my wife's family. I answered yes, though I knew of none; but I disliked saying that I myself had nearly died of the disease, and that before nursing me Marceline had never been ill. And I blamed everything on the embolism, although the doctor insisted on regarding it as no more than an incidental cause, and assured me that the disease had set in earlier. He urgently prescribed the pure air of the high Alps, where Marceline, he promised, would recover; and since as it happened my own preference was to spend the whole winter in the Engadine, once Marceline was well enough to bear the traveling we set out once again.

I remember as *events* each sensation of that journey.

The weather was clear and cold; we had brought our warmest furs with us. At Coire, the endless racket in the hotel kept us awake almost the whole night. For my part I could have cheerfully endured a sleepless night without feeling particularly tired; but Marceline . . . And I was infuriated not so much by the noise as by the fact that she could not sleep despite it. She needed sleep so badly! The next day we left before dawn; we had reserved seats in the Coire diligence; the relays were arranged so that we could reach Saint-Moritz in one day.

Tiefenkasten, the Julier, Samaden . . . I remember it all, hour by hour; the unexpected harsh quality of the air; the sound of the harness bells; my hunger; the midday stop at an inn; the raw egg I broke into the soup, the dark bread and the cold sour wine. Such coarse fare didn't suit Marceline; she could eat virtually nothing but a few biscuits I had luckily thought to bring along for the journey. I remember the sunset that day, the shadow rising fast on the wooded slopes; then another stop. The air grew constantly sharper, harsher. When the diligence stopped, we were plunged into the heart of darkness, and into a limpid silence; limpid . . . there is no other word. The least sound, against that strange transparency, took on its perfect quality, its consummate resonance. We set out again by night. Marceline coughed . . . Oh would she never stop coughing? I remembered the Sousse diligence: it seemed to me I had coughed better than that. She made too much of an effort . . . How weak she seemed, how changed; there in the darkness I scarcely recognized her. How drawn her features were! Did the two black holes of her nostrils always look like that? —She coughed horribly. And that was the best result of all her care. I detest sympathy; every infection is hidden within it; only the strong deserve sympathy. —Oh how could she bear any more! Would we never get there? . . . What was she doing? . . . She took her handkerchief, raised it to her lips, turned away . . . My God, was it her turn to spit blood now? —Brutally I tore the handkerchief out of her hands. In the faint light from the lantern . . . nothing. But I had betrayed my fear; sadly Marceline made herself smile and murmured: "No, not yet."

Finally we arrived. Just in time: she was scarcely alive. The rooms reserved for us were not satisfactory; they would do for the night, but we must have better ones the next day. Nothing seemed good enough, nothing too expensive. And because the winter season had not yet begun, the enormous hotel was virtually empty; I had my choice. We moved into two spacious rooms, bright and simply furnished, opening off a large sitting room with a broad bay window from which we could see both the hideous blue lake and some brutal mountain peak, its slopes either too thickly wooded or too bare. Here we would take our meals. The apartment was an extravagance, but what did I care! It was true I no longer had my lectures, but I was selling La Morinière. And then we would see. Besides, what did I need money for? Why did I need all this? I was strong now. A reversal of fortune, I decided, should teach as much as a reversal of health. Marceline of course required luxury; she was weak. Oh, for her I would spend so much, so much that . . . And I was filled with both the loathing and the love of such luxury. I bathed in it, steeped my sensuality in it, then wanted that sensuality to turn vagabond.

Meanwhile Marceline was improving, and my constant care was showing good results. Because she found it difficult to eat, I ordered dainty, delectable meals to stimulate her appetite; we drank the best wines. I persuaded myself that she too was fond of them, so much pleasure did I take in the exotic vintages we sampled every day—sharp Rhine wines, almost syrupy Tokays which dazed me with their heady power. I remember a strange Barba-Grisca of which only one bottle was left, so that I never knew if others would have had the same incongruous taste.

Every day we took a drive, first in a carriage, then, once the snow had fallen, in a sledge, bundled up to the chin in furs. I came back with my face glowing, famished, then sleepy. Yet I hadn't completely abandoned my work, and managed to find an hour or two every day in which to think over what I felt obliged to say. By then there was no question of history; historical research had long since ceased to interest me except as a means of

91

psychological investigation. I have said how much the past had attracted me all over again, once I imagined I saw certain disturbing analogies in it; I had actually supposed that by questioning the dead I might obtain the secret of life itself. But now, if young Athalaric himself had risen from his grave to speak to me, I would not have listened to the past. How could an old answer have satisfied my new question: What more can man do, what else can man be? That was what I had to know. Was what man had said up till then all he *could* say? Wasn't there something he didn't know about himself? Could he merely repeat himself? . . . And day by day there grew within me the confused sense of untapped wealth lying hidden, smothered by culture, propriety, rules.

I began to feel I had been born to make undreamed-of discoveries; and I grew almost fanatical in my quest, for whose sake I realized the seeker must abjure, must disdain culture, propriety, rules.

I reached the point of enjoying in others only the wildest behavior, deploring whatever constraint inhibited any excess. I came close to regarding honesty itself as no more than restriction, convention, timidity. I would have preferred cherishing it as something rare and arduous; our manners had made it into no more than an ordinary contract. In Switzerland, honesty is no more than a kind of comfort. I realized that Marceline needed such comfort, yet I didn't conceal from her my new train of thought. When, as early as Neuchâtel, she would praise the honesty which seeped out of the walls, out of the faces:

"My own's enough for me," I sneered. "I can't bear honest people. If I have nothing to fear from them, I have nothing to learn either. And what have they to say for themselves . . . ? The honest Swiss! All their prosperity is worthless. Without crimes, without history, without literature, without art, what are they but an overgrown rosebush that bears neither thorns nor bloom!"

That this honest country would bore me I knew before I arrived in it, but after two months this boredom of mine became a kind of frenzy, and I thought of nothing but leaving.

It was now mid-January. Marceline was better, much better: the low-grade fever that had been slowly under-mining her health had fallen at last; a fresher blood brought new color to her cheeks; once again she enjoyed walking, though only a little while at a time; no longer was she constantly tired, as she had been. I had no great difficulty convincing her that she had acquired all the benefit this tonic air could impart; that nothing would be better for her now than a trip down to Italy, where the warm favor of the spring would complete her convalescence—and above all I had no great difficulty convincing myself, so weary was I of the heights.

And yet now, when in my idleness the hated past regains its power, these are just the memories which obsess me. Flying sleigh rides, the joyous sting of the dry air, the spattering snow, appetite; groping ventures into the mist, strange sonorities of voices, the sudden looming-up of objects; reading in the snug sitting room, the landscape through the window—the icy landscape; the agonizing suspense of the snow, the disappearance of the outer world; the voluptuous huddle of my thoughts . . . Oh to skate with her once more down there, alone on that pure little lake among the larches, alone; then to come back together, in the evening . . .

Our descent into Italy gave me all the vertigo of falling. The weather was beautiful. As we advanced into a warmer, denser air, the stiff trees of the peaks, orderly larches and firs, gave way to a vegetation rich with soft grace, with ease. I seemed to be abandoning abstractions in favor of life, and though it was winter still, I kept imagining perfumes in the air. For too long, now, our only laughter had been at shadows! My privation intoxicated me, and it was on thirst that I was drunk, as others get drunk on wine. The temperance of my life had been admirable; on the threshold of this tolerant and promising land, all my appetites exploded. An enormous reservoir of love overflowed within me, surging from deep in my flesh up to my brain, deluging my thoughts.

This illusion of spring did not last long. The sudden change of altitude may have troubled me momentarily, but once we left the sheltered shores of the lakes, Bellagio and Como, where we had lingered for several days, we returned to winter and rain. We both began to suffer from the cold, which we had borne easily in the Engadine; it was no longer dry and light, as on the heights, but damp and gloomy there, and Marceline began to cough again. To escape, we journeyed farther south: we left Milan for Florence, Florence for Rome, Rome for Naples—in the winter rains, Naples is the most lugubrious city I know. I have never been so bored in my life. We returned to Rome, seeking if not warmth at least a vestige of comfort. On the Pincio we rented an apartment that was too large for us, but splendidly situated. Even before, in Florence, tired of hotels, we had rented an exquisite villa on the Viale dei Celli for three months. Anyone else would have longed to live there forever; we stayed no more than three weeks. Yet at each new stop I insisted on arranging everything as if we would never leave. A stronger demon drove me on. Add to this that we lugged around no fewer than eight trunks. One, full of nothing but books, I never opened during the entire trip.

I refused to tell Marceline how much we were spending or make any attempt to economize, though of course I knew such extravagances could not last. I ceased to count on the money from La Morinière; the place no longer brought in any income, and Bocage wrote that he couldn't find a buyer. Yet each consideration of the future led only to more spending. What need would I have of so much money once I was alone, I would think, and filled with anguish and expectation I watched Marceline's fragile life diminish even faster than my fortune.

Though she relied on me to make every arrangement, these abrupt moves exhausted her; yet what wearied her even more, I now dare admit, was the fear of what was in my mind. "I see what it is," she said to me one day, "I understand your . . . doctrine—for that's what it is now, a doctrine. It may be beautiful," and then she added in a lower tone, wistfully: "but it eliminates the weak."

"As it should," I blurted out in spite of myself.

Then, under the impact of my brutal words, I seemed to feel this delicate creature shudder and shrink away from me. Oh, perhaps you think I didn't love Marceline. I swear, I loved her passionately. Never had she been, and never had she seemed to me, so lovely. Illness had refined and actually exalted her features. I almost never left her now, surrounded her with continuous care, protected, watched over her every moment of the day and night. However light her sleep, I trained my own to be lighter still; I waited till she dropped off and made sure to waken before her. When sometimes I left her for an hour to take a walk by myself in the country or in the streets, a loving anxiety, a fear she might be bored, quickly brought me back to her; then sometimes I steeled my will and protested against this power, castigating myself: is this all you are worth, fake master of men!—and forced myself to stay away longer. But then I would return, my arms filled with flowers, early garden flowers or hothouse blossoms . . . Yes, I tell you I loved her dearly. But how can I express this—that insofar as I respected myself less I revered her more—and who's to say how many passions and how many warring thoughts can cohabit in a man? . . .

The bad weather was long past; the season was advancing; and suddenly the almond trees bloomed. On the morning of the first of March I went down into the Piazza di Spagna: peasants had stripped the Campagna of its white branches, and almond blossoms filled the flower vendors' baskets. I was so delighted that I bought a whole grove of them. Three men carried them home for me; I came in with all this springtime: branches caught at the doors, petals snowed on the carpet. I put them everywhere, in all the vases; while Marceline was out of the living room for a moment I turned it white with their bloom. Already I rejoiced in her pleasure; I heard her coming. Here she was. She opened the door. What was the matter with her? . . . She reeled . . . She burst out crying.

"What's wrong, my poor darling? . . ." I rushed to her, covered her with tender caresses.

Then, as if to justify her tears: "Those flowers—the scent makes me ill," she said.

And it was such a faint, reticent odor of honey. Without a word I snatched up those innocent, delicate branches, broke them into pieces, carried them outside, threw them away, furious, my eyes burning. —If even this little bit of spring was too much for her! . . .

I often recall those tears, and I realize now she must have known she was doomed: Marceline was mourning other springtimes. I suppose too that there are strong joys for the strong, and weak joys for the weak who would be injured by the stronger ones. Marceline was overwhelmed by the mildest enjoyment; anything more intense was intolerable to her. What she called happiness I called rest, and I neither could nor would rest.

Four days later, we set out again for Sorrento. I was disappointed to find it no warmer. Everything seemed to be shivering. The endless wind tormented Marceline. We had wanted to stay at the same hotel as on our first trip; we took the very room. We stared with amazement, under that leaden sky, at the whole disenchanted scene, and at the hotel's dreary garden which had seemed so charming to us when our love strolled there.

We decided to take a boat to Palermo, whose climate was spoken of so favorably, and went back to Naples, where we were to embark and where we stayed on a few days longer. But in Naples at least I wasn't bored. Naples is a lively city where the past is not a tyrant.

Almost every minute of the day I spent with Marceline. At night she went to bed early, exhausted; I would wait until she fell asleep, and sometimes went to bed myself; then, when her more regular breathing indicated she was asleep, I would noiselessly get up, dress again in the dark and slip outside like a thief.

Outside—oh, I could have shouted with pleasure! What would I do now? I didn't even know. The sky, overcast all day, was cleared of its clouds; the nearly full moon glowed. I walked at random, without purpose, without desire, without constraint. I looked at everything with fresh eyes, lay in wait for each noise with more attentive ears; I savored the moisture of the night; I rested my hand upon things; I prowled.

The last night of our stay in Naples, I prolonged this

vagrant debauch. When at last I came in I found Marceline in tears. She had been frightened, she told me, suddenly waking and no longer feeling me beside her. I calmed her, explained my absence as best I could and resolved not to leave her again. But the very first night in Palermo I broke my resolution and went out. The first orange trees were in bloom; the faintest breath of air carried their scent.

We stayed only five days in Palermo; then, by a long detour, returned to Taormina, which we both wanted to see again. Have I said that the village is perched high up on the mountainside? The station is down at sea level. The carriage which drove us up to the hotel had to take me back down to the station for our trunks. I stood up in the carriage to talk to the driver, a boy from Catania, lovely as a line of Theocritus, vivid, scented, savory as a fruit.

"Com'è bella la signora!" he said in a charming voice, watching Marceline walk away.

"Anche tu sei bello, ragazzo," I answered; and as I was leaning toward him, I couldn't resist my impulse, and abruptly drawing him against me, kissed him. He yielded with a laugh. *"I Francesi sono tutti amanti,"* he said.

"Ma non tutti gli Italiani amati," I replied, laughing too. I looked for him on the following days, but never managed to see him again.

We left Taormina for Syracuse. Step by step we were retracing, in reverse, our first journey, turning back toward the dawn of our love. And just as from week to week, during our first journey, I had advanced toward recovery, so from week to week, as we moved southward, Marceline's condition grew worse.

By what aberration, what stubborn blindness, what deliberate folly did I convince myself and above all try to convince her that she must have still more light and warmth, invoking the memory of my own convalescence in Biskra? . . . Yet the air had grown warmer; the bay of Palermo is a mild place, and Marceline enjoyed it. There, perhaps, she might have . . . But was I free to choose what I wanted, to decide what I desired?

In Syracuse, the state of the sea and the irregular boat service forced us to wait eight days. Every moment I didn't spend with Marceline I spent in the old port. That tiny harbor of Syracuse! the smells of rancid wine, muddy alleys, the stinking tavern crowded with stevedores, tramps, drunken sailors. The dregs of society were delectable company to me, and what need had I of understanding their speech when my whole body savored it! Here too the brutality of passion assumed in my eyes a hypocritical aspect of health, of vigor. It was no use reminding myself that their wretched lives could not have for them the savor they assumed for me . . . I actually longed to roll under the table with them and waken only with the sad shudders of dawn. Among these men I aggravated my growing horror of luxury, of comfort, of what I had surrounded myself with, of that protection my new health had made useless, of all those precautions one takes to preserve one's body from the dangerous contact of life. I imagined their existence elsewhere, longed to follow them, to penetrate deeper into their drunkenness . . . Then suddenly I had a vision of Marceline . . . What was she doing at that moment? Suffering, crying perhaps . . . I leaped up and ran back to the hotel, over whose door seemed written the words: No Poor Man Enters Here.

Marceline always greeted me in the same way: without a word of reproach or doubt, and striving despite everything to smile. We took our meals in our room; I ordered for her the best food our mediocre hotel could provide. And during the meal I kept thinking: a piece of bread, of cheese, a stalk of fennel is enough for *them* and would be enough for me too. And perhaps back there, quite close by, some of them are going hungry, some of them lack even that much, while here on my table is enough to glut them for three days! I longed to knock down the walls, to summon my guests to their feast. The realization that others were starving became for me a dreadful anguish. And I went back down to the harbor, where I handed out at random the coins with which I had filled my pockets.

Human poverty is an enslavement; to eat, a poor man consents to joyless labor, and all labor which is not joyous is mere drudgery, I thought. I would pay one man after another to rest, saying, "Stop working—you hate what you're doing." For each man I desired that leisure without which nothing new can flower—neither vice nor art.

Marceline made no mistake about what was on my mind; when I returned from the harbor I didn't deceive her about what sort of pathetic creatures surrounded me there. Everything is within Man. She sensed already what I was struggling to discover; and when I reproached her for believing too often in the virtues she herself had invented in the people we knew, she replied: "You're never satisfied until you've made them reveal some vice. Don't you realize that our own eyes magnify and exaggerate whatever they happen to see—that we make anyone become what we claim he is?"

I might have wished she were wrong, but I had to admit that to me each man's worst instinct seemed the most sincere. Then, what was it I called sincerity?

At last we left Syracuse. I was obsessed by my memory and longing for the South. Once on the water, Marceline felt better . . . I can still see the color of the Mediterranean, which was so calm the ship's wake seemed to linger in it. I can hear the sounds—dripping, liquid sounds; the washing of the deck and the slapping of the sailors' bare feet on the planks. I can see Malta, dead white; the approach to Tunis . . . How I have changed!

It is hot. It is beautiful. Everything is splendid. If only, in each sentence I speak here, a whole harvest of pleasure could be distilled! There's no use attempting now to impose more order on my story than there was in my life then. I've been trying long enough to tell you how I became what I am. If only I could rid my mind of this unendurable logic! . . . I feel nothing in myself except nobility.

Tunis. Light. A light not so much powerful as plentiful. Even the shadows are full of light. The air itself seems a luminous fluid in which everything steeps—you dive into it, you swim through it. This land of pleasure satisfies without calming desire; indeed, every satisfaction merely exalts it.

A land liberated from works of art. I despise those who can acknowledge beauty only when it's already transcribed, interpreted. One thing admirable about the Arabs: they live their art, they sing and scatter it from day to day; they don't cling to it, they don't embalm it in *works*. Which is the cause and the effect of the absence of great artists. I have always believed the great artists are the ones who dare *entitle to beauty* things so natural that when they're seen afterward people say: Why did I never realize before that this too was beautiful? . . .

At Kairouan, which I hadn't yet seen and which I visited without Marceline, the night was clear and mild. Just as I was returning to the hotel, I remembered a group of Arabs I had noticed lying in the open air on the mats of a little café. I went and slept among them. I returned covered with vermin.

Because the humidity of the coast greatly weakened Marceline, I persuaded her that we must get to Biskra as soon as possible. That was the beginning of April.

This trip is a very long one. The first day, we reached Constantine without a halt; the second day, Marceline was so tired that we went no farther than El Kantara. There we sought, and toward evening found, a shade cooler and more delicious than even moonlight—it was like an inexhaustible draught which streamed toward us, and from the slope where we were sitting we could see the whole plain aglow with the sunset. That night Marceline couldn't sleep; the strangeness of the silence and of the least sounds disturbed her. I was afraid she had a touch of fever. I heard her stirring on her bed. The next morning she looked paler to me. We set out again.

Biskra. Here then was my destination. Yes; here was the park; the bench . . . I recognized the bench where I used to sit during the first days of my convalescence. What was I reading then? . . . Homer, which I hadn't opened since. —Here was the tree whose bark I had stood up to feel. How weak I was then! . . . And now, here were the children . . . No, I recognized none of them.

How serious Marceline looked! She had changed as much as I. Why was she coughing, in this beautiful weather? —Here was the hotel; here were our rooms, our veranda. —What was Marceline thinking? She hadn't spoken a word. —As soon as she reached her room, she stretched out on the bed; she was exhausted and said she wanted to sleep a little. I went outside.

I didn't recognize the children, but the children recognized me. Informed of my arrival, they all came running to meet me. Could these be the right ones? The disappointment! What had happened? They had grown up— hideously . . . In just over two years—could it be possible? . . . What exhaustion, what vices, what sloth had already imprinted such ugliness on these faces in which so much youth once had bloomed? What servile labors had warped these lovely bodies so quickly? It was a kind of bankruptcy . . . I asked questions. Bachir was washing dishes in a café; Ashour earned a few sous breaking stones on the highway; Hammatar had lost an eye. Who would have believed it: Sadeck had reformed; he was helping an older brother sell bread in the market; he seemed to have lost his wits. Agib had become a butcher, like his father; he was overweight now, ugly, rich, and no longer spoke to his *déclassé* companions . . . How stupid respectability makes a man! Would I find among these boys just what I most hated at home? —Boubaker? Married. Not yet fifteen. Grotesque! —No, not quite—I saw him that evening and he explained: the marriage was merely a pretense; he had become, I suspect, an utter good-for-nothing. He drank, and already was losing his looks . . . And was this all that remained? All that life had made of them? —I realized from my unbearable sadness that *these* were the real reason I had returned to Biskra—Ménalque was right: Memory is an invention of misery.

And Moktir? —Ah, Moktir had just left prison. He was lying low. The rest no longer had anything to do with him. I asked to see him again. He was the handsomest of them all; would he disappoint me too? . . . He was found, brought to see me. No! this one hadn't failed me. Even my memory hadn't pictured him so splendid: his strength and his beauty were fulfilled, perfect. Recognizing me, he smiled.

"What did you do to get thrown into prison, Moktir?"

"Nothing."

"Were you stealing?"

He protested.

"What are you doing now?"

He smiled.

"Well, Moktir, if you have nothing to do, you can come with us to Touggourt." And I was suddenly seized by a longing to go to Touggourt.

Marceline wasn't feeling well; I couldn't tell what was happening to her. When I returned to the hotel that evening, she pressed against me without a word, eyes closed. Her wide sleeve slid up, revealing her shrunken arm. I caressed her, cradled her in my arms for a long while, like a child I was rocking to sleep. Was it love, or anguish, or fever that made her tremble that way? . . . Oh, perhaps there would still be time . . . Would nothing stop me? I had sought and found what makes me what I am: a kind of persistence in the worst. —But how did I bring myself to tell Marceline that the next day we would be leaving for Touggourt? . . .

She was asleep in the next room. The moon, long since risen, flooded the terrace, almost terrifyingly bright. There was no escaping it. My bedroom had a white tile floor, and the moon glowed whiter still upon it, pouring through the open windows. I recognized that brilliance in the room, the shadow of the door cast upon it. Two years before, it had reached still farther—yes, *there* where it had moved now—when I had got out of bed, unable to sleep. I had leaned against that same door jamb. I recognized the motionless palms . . . What words had I been reading that night? . . . Oh, yes; Christ's words to Peter: "Now thou girdest thyself and goest where thou wouldst . . ." Where was I going now? Where did I want to go? . . . I didn't tell you that from Naples, that last time, I had gone to Paestum one day, alone . . . Oh, I could have sobbed before those stones! The ancient beauty appeared: simple, perfect, smiling—abandoned. Art is leaving me, I feel it. To make room for . . . what? No longer, as before, a smiling harmony . . . I no longer know, now, the dark god I serve. O new God! Grant that I may yet know new races, unforeseen kinds of beauty.

The next day, at dawn, we left in the diligence. Moktir was with us. Moktir was happy as a king.

Chegga; Kefeldorh'; M'reyer . . . Dismal stages on the still more dismal, interminable road. I confess I had expected these oases to be more inviting—more than stone and sand and at best a few stunted bushes with curious blossoms; sometimes a scattering of palms, nourished by a hidden spring . . . To such oases I now prefer the desert—a land of deadly glory and intolerable splendor. Here man's effort seems ugly and miserable. These days, every other part of the earth bores me.

"You love the inhuman," Marceline said. But how she herself stared—with what hunger!

The weather changed for the worse the next day; that is, the wind rose and the horizon dimmed. Marceline was suffering; the sand in the air burned her skin, irritated her throat; the excessive light tired her eyes; this hostile landscape was torturing her. But it was too late to turn back now. In a few hours we would be in Touggourt.

It is this last part of the journey, close to me though it still is, that I remember least. Impossible, now, to recall the scenery of that second day and what I did once we reached Touggourt. But what I do remember still is my impatience and my haste.

It had been very cold in the morning. Toward evening, a burning simoom came up. Marceline, exhausted by the journey, had gone to bed as soon as we arrived. I had hoped to find a somewhat more comfortable hotel; our room was dreadful; the sand, the sun and the flies had soiled whatever they had not already faded and worn. Having eaten almost nothing since dawn, I ordered our dinner at once; but nothing seemed appetizing to Marceline, and I could not persuade her to eat a mouthful. We had brought tea things with us, and I busied myself with these paltry tasks: we improvised a dinner out of some biscuits and this tea, whose taste was ruined by the briny water of the region.

By a last pretense of virtue, I stayed with her until evening. And suddenly I too felt at the end of my strength. O taste of ashes! O weariness! The misery of that superhuman effort! I scarcely dared look at Marceline; I knew all too well that my eyes, instead of trying to meet hers, would slide down to the black holes of her nostrils; the expression of her sickly face was excruciating. Nor did she look at me. I felt her anguish as if I were touching it. She coughed a great deal; then fell asleep. Every now and then a sudden spasm shook her body.

Perhaps the night would be a bad one—before it was too late, I wanted to know where I could find help. I went out. In front of the hotel door, the square, the streets, the very atmosphere, were all so alien that I could scarcely believe what I saw and heard. After a few moments I went back inside. Marceline was sleeping calmly. I had been mistaken to be alarmed; in this fantastic country, dangers seemed to lurk everywhere; it was ridiculous. And, sufficiently reassured, I went out again.

How strange the nocturnal animation of the square; a silent traffic—the clandestine gliding of white *burnous*. Every other moment, a burst of strange music vanished on the breeze. Someone came toward me . . . It was Moktir. He had been waiting for me, he said, and was sure I would come back out. He laughed. He knew Touggourt, came here often, and wanted to take me somewhere. I let him lead me away.

We walked in the dark until we reached a Moorish café; this was where the music came from. Some Arab women were dancing—if you could call their monotonous gliding a dance. —One of them took my hand; I followed her; it was Moktir's mistress; he came too. The three of us went into a long, narrow room whose sole piece of furniture was a very low bed on which we all sat down. A white rabbit, shut up in the room, shrank away from us at first, then came up and nibbled out of Moktir's hand. Coffee was brought in. Then, while Moktir played with the rabbit, this woman drew me to her, and I yielded to her embrace the way you give yourself up to sleep.

Oh, here I might lie to you or simply keep silent; but

what would this story of mine matter to me if it were no longer the truth?

I returned alone to the hotel—Moktir remained where we had been for what was left of the night. It was late. A dry sirocco was blowing—a wind heavy with sand and scorching, despite the darkness; a feverish wind, blinding, hard to walk against; but suddenly I was frantic to get back, and I reached the hotel almost at a run. Perhaps she had awakened; perhaps she needed me? . . . No; the window of our room was dark; she was asleep. I waited for the wind to die down before I opened the door; I walked very softly into the dark room. —What was that noise? . . . I didn't recognize her cough . . . Could that be Marceline? . . . I put on the light . . .

She was half sitting up on her bed; was clutching at the bars of the bed with one of her thin arms to hold herself up; her sheets, her hands, her nightgown glistened with a stream of blood; her face was smeared with it; her eyes were staring, hideously wide; and no cry of agony would have horrified me so much as her silence. I searched her dripping face for a place to deposit one dreadful kiss; the taste of her perspiration clung to my lips. I bathed and cooled her forehead, her cheeks. Against the bed, something hard under my foot; I bent down and picked up the little rosary she had asked for once in Paris; she had dropped it; I slipped it into her open hand, but just then her hand went limp, and the rosary fell again. I didn't know what to do; I wanted to run for help . . . Her hand clung to me desperately, holding me; ah, she thought I wanted to leave her now, that was it! She said: "Oh, can't you wait a little longer?" Then she saw I wanted to speak to her. "Don't say anything," she added, "everything's all right."

Again I picked up the rosary and put it back in her hand, but again it slipped out—what am I saying? she deliberately dropped it. I knelt beside her and pressed her hand in mine.

She sank back, half against the bolster and half against my shoulder, apparently asleep, though her eyes remained wide open.

An hour later she sat up again; her hand released

105

mine, clutched at her nightgown and tore the lace. She was choking. —Toward dawn she vomited blood again.

I have finished telling you my story. What else is there for me to say? —The French cemetery in Touggourt is hideous, half devoured by the sand . . . What little will power I had left I used up getting her out of that terrible place. Marceline lies buried at El Kantara, in the shade of a private garden she used to like. All this happened scarcely three months ago. These three months have done the work of ten years.

Michel remained silent for a long time. We too said nothing, each of us struck dumb by a strange uneasiness. We felt, alas, that by relating it, Michel had somehow legitimized his action. Not knowing where to object to it, in his gradual accounting, made us almost . . . accomplices. We were somehow involved in it. He had completed his story without a quaver in his voice, without an inflection or a gesture to reveal that any emotion whatever disturbed him, either because he took a cynical pride in not seeming moved, or because a kind of reticence kept him from moving us by his tears, or because he simply wasn't moved. I can't distinguish in him, even now, what is pride, or strength, or aridity, or reserve. —After a moment he went on:

What alarms me, I confess, is that I'm still quite young. Sometimes it seems to me as if my real life hasn't begun yet. Tear me away from this place now, give me some reason to live. I myself no longer know where to look. I may have liberated myself, but what does it matter? This useless freedom tortures me. It's not—believe me, it's not that I'm tired of my crime, if that's what you want to call it; but I must prove to myself that I have not exceeded my rights.

When you first knew me, I had a great steadfastness of mind, and I know that's what makes real men—I have it no longer. But this climate, I believe, is what's responsible for the change. Nothing discourages thought so much as this perpetual blue sky. Here any exertion is impossible, so closely does pleasure follow desire. Surrounded by splendor and by death, I feel happiness too close, and the surrender to it too constant. I lie down in the middle of the day to deceive the dreary prospect of time and its intolerable leisure. I keep here, look! some white pebbles that I leave in the shade to steep, then I hold them a long time in the palm of my hand, until the soothing coolness they've borrowed is . . . used up. Then I begin again, alternating the stones, putting back in the shade the ones whose coolness has been exhausted. That's how time passes, and evening comes . . . Drag me away from here; I can't leave of my own accord. Something in my will has been broken; I don't even know where I found the strength to leave El Kantara. Sometimes I'm afraid that what I have suppressed will take its revenge. I want to make a fresh start. I want to get rid of what remains of my fortune; look, these walls are still covered with it. I live here on almost nothing. A half-caste innkeeper cooks what little I need. The child you frightened away when you came brings it to me morning and night in exchange for a few sous and a few caresses. He turns shy with strangers, but with me he's as affectionate and faithful as a dog. His sister's an Ouled-Naïl—each winter she goes back to Constantine and sells her body to anyone who wants it. She's quite pretty and sometimes, during those first weeks, I let her spend the night with me. But one morning her brother, little Ali, surprised us in bed together. He seemed very angry, and wouldn't come back for five days. Yet he knows perfectly well how and on what his sister lives; he used to speak of it before without the slightest embarrassment. Was he jealous, then? —In any case, the rascal got his way, for half out of boredom, half out of fear of losing Ali, I haven't had the girl here again ever since. She didn't mind that, but each time I see her she laughs and claims I prefer the boy to her. She claims he's what keeps me here more than anything else. There may be some truth in what she says . . .

The Immoralist: An Interpretation

In personal terms, *L'Immoraliste* was a symbolic act of dissociation from Michel. Had Gide not discovered himself so fully, he too might have been driven to such a harsh and aimless individualism. This is the book's "personal" subject. *L'Immoraliste* is also, of course, a critique (not rejection) of Nietzschean individualism. But most of all it is a study of latent homosexuality, of repression and compensation, of the effect preconscious energies may have on a man's acts, feelings, and ideas. It is no wonder, since the book was all these things, that it was little read and little understood at first. A very few early readers—and readers as different as Madame Rachilde and Francis Jammes—saw that the conflict was a sexual one. Yet Lilian Neguloa's valuable census shows that a large majority of the book's critics (including some very recent ones) have considered *L'Immoraliste* to be a novel "about individualism" and have not seen Michel's homosexuality at all. Some, to be sure, may have simply refused to acknowledge what they saw. Thus Charles du Bos candidly admits that he could not take up "le problème Wilde" with the particular audience of his early lecture on the book. Unlike French biography, French criticism has long resisted the influence of psychology and has also remained curiously discreet.

There is the further fact that Michel's revolt against repression and conformity may be transferred to any plane of experience, and so may invite the sympathy of a critic differently repressed. But the strongest obstacle to understanding has probably been the inveterate tendency of critics to take a narrative told in the first person at its face value and to confuse the narrator's consciousness with the author's. It is nevertheless hard to understand why so few critics (including those who return constantly to "intention") have referred to Gide's recognition that Michel was an unconscious homosexual. Miss Neguloa's article reminds us that nearly all readers are casual readers, and that most criticism of fiction is inexpert to an unsuspected and scandalous degree. It also suggests that any new commentary on *L'Immoraliste* must, to counteract established misconception, provide an old-fashioned summary of plot.

Michel, a precocious and withdrawn archaeologist of twenty-four, marries Marceline to please his dying father. At first he hardly realizes that she is a human being, with an inner life of her own. He feels at most tenderness and pity, and the honeymoon is loveless in every sense. Michel's long accumulated fatigue brings on tuberculosis. He begins to spit blood while crossing the desert and arrives at Biskra more dead than alive. His first surrender to sickness is followed by a violent craving to live. To consider as "right" only what contributes to health is the first phase of his "immoralism." And as health returns he begins to suspect that life has unexplored joys, that he carries within him a precious and unrealized self. He determines to discover this self by a ruthless elimination of everything factitious and acquired.* The self is a palimpsest. All the false superscriptions of education and moral training must be erased before he can discover the "occult text."

Marceline unwittingly takes the first important step toward revelation. She brings Bachir, a handsome native

---

* Michel's sickness and convalescence recalls Nietzsche's as well as Gide's, as this striking parallel shows: "After that touch from the wing of Death, what seemed important is so no longer; other things become so which had at first seemed unimportant, or which one did not even know existed. The miscellaneous mass of acquired knowledge of every kind that has overlain the mind gets pulled off in places like a mask of paint, exposing the bare skin—the very flesh of the authentic creature that had lain beneath it" (*The Immoralist* [New York, 1930], p. 64). "Illness likewise gave me the right to a complete reversal of my mode of life; it not only allowed, it actually ordered me to forget; it enforced the necessity of repose, of idleness, of waiting, of patience . . . And all that meant thinking! . . . The state of my eyes was enough to stop all book-wormishness, or, in plain English, philology: I was delivered from books; for years I read nothing—the greatest boon I have ever conferred upon myself! That essential self, which had been buried, as it were, which had lost its voice under the pressure of being forced to listen to other selves continually (which is what reading means!), awakened slowly, timidly, doubtfully—but at last it *spoke again*" ("Ecce Homo," translated by Clifton Fadiman, *The Philosophy of Nietzsche* [Modern Library edition], pp. 84–85).

110

child, to Michel's sickroom. Michel interprets his affection for the boy as a love of animal health. But when he is able to go outside and watch the children at play, he is irritated by his wife's presence. He is "frightened" by the weak, sickly, and well-behaved boys she brings to their rooms but fascinated by the unruly Moktir. He says nothing when he sees Moktir steal a pair of scissors. And now he invents various pretexts for seeing the boys alone: Ashour, Lassif, and Lachmi with his "golden nudity." He wanders into one particular enchanted garden which will haunt his memory, and perhaps account for the attraction shaded places are to hold for him in Ravello and Normandy. But as the hot days approach they leave Biskra and the children behind. Michel feels that his love for Marceline is increasing, yet he takes pleasure in concealing from her his sense of a hidden, undefined self. In Italy, on the way back to France and a resumption of his studies, he has a fight with a drunken coachman. That night he possesses Marceline for the first time.

Michel leads a curiously divided life during the months that follow. On the one hand he tries to impose order on La Morinière, his Norman estate. He guards against "vagabond inclination" by tying himself down to an expensive Paris apartment, and by accepting a lectureship at the College de France. But he is attracted in his studies only by barbarism and indiscipline; by such figures as the fifteen-year-old Athalaric, in revolt against his mother and his Latin education. His lectures become an "apology and eulogy of nonculture." His friend Ménalque (who had visited Biskra after him and had heard of his liking for the native children) demands an explanation of these contradictions. Is Michel one of those who, out of a fear of isolation, refuse to be themselves? Before leaving on another of his fabulous journeys, Ménalque preaches the joys of dangerous living; that is, of the acceptance of life as it comes.

The balance between anarchy and discipline wavers during the months which separate the two visits to La Morinière. Something, seemingly Ménalque's lessons, tips it sharply toward anarchy. On the first visit Michel had spent his days supervising his estate with the prudent and orderly Charles, the caretaker's seventeen-year-old son. But now he is fascinated by the most primitive and irresponsible of the farmhands; feels an "evil curiosity" concerning them. He takes up with Bute, a demoralized army veteran, and listens avidly to his stories of the incestuous Heurtevents. He catches the boy Alcide poaching, and joins him in poaching on his own estate. He now feels a strange urge to destroy the harmony and order he had helped establish. He tries in vain to spend more time with his wife, who had lost a child, and who has begun to show tubercular symptoms. His pity struggles against a deepening sense that she is tainted by this illness. Her weakness seems contemptible.

Michel sells La Morinière and takes Marceline to St. Moritz. But he is intolerably bored by the honest mediocrity of the Swiss. His "reverence" for his wife increases simultaneously with a now demonic urge to spend all his money; to move always farther to the south; to seek out and observe, in each Italian city, the "lowest dregs of humanity." In Taormina he feels an irresistible attraction for a coachman—a Sicilian boy "as beautiful as a line of Theocritus"—and kisses him. A few days later they leave for Syracuse, and here too Michel neglects his dying wife to seek out the sailors and vagabonds in the port cafés. But Syracuse is only a last and futile detour. Their destination is Biskra. This time when they arrive it is Marceline who is more dead than alive.

In the two years, the native children have changed horribly. Only Moktir, just out of prison, remains "superb." In his vague restlessness Michel drags his wife on to Touggourt, taking Moktir with them. On the first night there he sleeps with Moktir's mistress in the boy's presence, seeking peace in highly cerebral perversion. He returns to the hotel in time to see Marceline die. Only then, freed from conscious restraint yet still restless, he sends for the three friends to whom he tells his story. Can they advise him? Tell him what to do with his objectless freedom? Even Michel is aware that this freedom is not truly complete. "Sometimes I am afraid that what I have suppressed will avenge itself." In the months since Marceline's death he has spent an occasional night with an Ouled

Naïl prostitute. But the girl suspects it is really her little brother Ali he desires. "Perhaps she is not altogether wrong . . ."

L'Immoraliste is one of the first modern novels to deal at all seriously with homosexuality. But it is most important to keep in mind that Michel never participates in a homosexual act. The reader who assumes that such acts occur but are not mentioned, for reasons of discretion, is likely to misinterpret everything else. One can imagine Gide's exasperation when Paul Bourget asked him, as late as 1915 (and as soon as Edith Wharton had left the room), whether Michel was a "practicing pederast." Through many pages of a first reading we have every right to share Michel's bewilderment. We explore him with the same curiosity that he explores himself. And how much would be lost if the last revealing lines of the novel were its first ones! But on second and subsequent readings the ambiguities should dissolve. Not till then, perhaps, does the reader notice that Michel possesses Marceline only after fighting with the drunken coachman; that he felt "obliged" (in an hour of frustration) to caress a strangely textured shrub; that his period of tranquillity at La Morinière ends abruptly with the coming of the boy Charles; that he longs to sleep in the barn because the boy Alcide sleeps there; that, in fact, he never proceeds beyond the stage of longing for these boys. The important fact about Michel is not that he is a homosexual, but that he is a latent homosexual, a homosexual without knowing it.

Thus *L'Immoraliste* is not a case study of a particular and manifest neurosis, but a story of unconscious repression. In the light of this, but only in this light, various unexplained ritual acts take on meaning: the shaving of the beard, or the ceremonial undressing, sun-bathing, and immersion in the pool near Ravello. The vengeance of what has been suppressed touches every fiber of Michel's intellectual and moral life; determines his self-destructiveness and his anti-intellectualism alike. Restrained from sexual satisfaction and even from self-discovery by an unconscious force, Michel rebels in other ways. The outburst may be sudden and specific, as when he leaps into

113

the draining lake and takes a savage excitement in catching eels with Charles. More generally, Michel rebels against his early intellectual training in his philosophical defense of barbarism; against his inherited Norman prudence in trying to destroy the harmony and order of his farm. *L'Immoraliste* dramatizes as clearly as Dostoevsky's *Gambler* the compulsion to risk—and lose. Payment must eventually be made to the internalized parental authority. But the first impulse is to destroy not appease this superego. The harshness of Michel's individualism—and this, in general terms, is no less than the "subject" of the novel—is determined by the harshness of the repression.

The hidden victim of this hidden restraint reveals itself in a curious hostility toward the convention-bound and in an abnormal sympathy for the free. Michel's acts seemed to many early readers (and even at times to himself) unmotivated and "Satanic." Like *The Secret Sharer, Heart of Darkness,* and parts of *Lord Jim, L'Immoraliste* dramatizes unconscious or half-conscious identification. The lawless buried self is attracted to all whom the superego and the waking conscience deem guilty, and repelled by all the well-behaved. Even when he is most determined to lead a regulated life, Michel's affections go out to the unmoral, the corrupt, the unrestrained. He has a "horror of honest folk," but is paralyzed by "joy" when he sees Moktir steal the scissors, when he learns that Alcide is a poacher—or when he uncovers, in the lifeless pages of his research, the youthful savagery of Athalaric. He envies Pierre's drunken brutality as he envies Ménalque's refined selfishness. The movement toward discovery is not, to be sure, uninterrupted. The alternating and sometimes simultaneous impulses to concentrate and to destroy the ego—to use Baudelaire's terminology rather than Freud's—increase or weaken according to the self at the moment dominant and the self at the moment suppressed. The frustrated Huguenot as well as the frustrated homosexual may demand satisfaction. In the final chapters, however, the inward aggressions become frenzied as the "authentic self" nears the surface.

Not all of Michel's feelings may be so simply explained.

Does he resent the dying Marceline because he fears a return of his own tuberculosis, or because he has equated weakness and virtue, or simply because he longs to be rid of her? One strength of *L'Immoraliste* lies in its awareness of the close interdependence of Michel's health, his degree of sexual adjustment, his moral heritage, and his intellectual interests. The novel's over-all "meaning" is reducible to the barest Freudian terms, but Michel as a character is not. His intelligence and will, however weak, do play some part. His tenderness toward Marceline develops into love at the same time as his cruelty toward her—and at the same time as his homosexual impulses. And if his ideas are determined by unconscious needs, his arguments still demand attention. The problem of individualism, though provoked in this instance by a specific sexual situation, nevertheless transcends neurosis.

For Gide knew that the problem of the emancipated individualist goes on, even after sexual adjustments have been made. Must one choose between a refusal to live and an individualism which makes others suffer? Marceline justly observes that Michel's doctrine may be a "fine one," but that it threatens to suppress the weak. And can the individualist cut himself off to be free, yet live in that rarefied air? "To know how to free oneself is nothing; the arduous thing is to know what to do with one's freedom." It is here, in its critique of Nietzschean individualism, that *L'Immoraliste* is necessarily imperfect —and first of all because Michel is an imperfect Nietzschean. Gide agreed with Michel and Nietzsche that the world is divided into the strong and the weak, and many of Michel's arguments are transcribed from *Les Nourritures terrestres*. But Michel was incapable of the solution Gide elsewhere proposed: to become fully conscious of the inner dialogue between order and anarchy, and to suppress by an act of will whichever voice threatens to become too strong. The very fact that makes Michel so interesting dramatically and psychologically—his imperfect understanding of himself—makes him a poor vehicle for Gidean and Nietzschean ideas. His story could not answer the question raised in the Prologue: how is society to use the energies of the free man? "I fear the failures of individualism," Gide wrote in 1898.* Michel is such a failure; he is not a free man.

Thus the aspect of *L'Immoraliste* most emphasized by critics is in fact unsatisfactory. The novel's strength lies rather in its art and psychological understanding, and in its controlled transposition of personal experience. For it is a "fruit filled with bitter ashes," a novel written severely from memory, but also out of mind and nerve. The triumph of intelligence reveals itself in the close pressure of form. Not a single irrelevant memory has survived this pressure, other than the memory of Wilde's epigrams. This required a conscious separation of the author's consciousness from Michel's, and a careful use of the "imperceptive" narrator as a technical device. We see in Rivière's *Aimée* and Chardonne's *Eva* (two books possibly derived from *L'Immoraliste*) to what diffuseness and incoherence this device may lead. Yet it remains one of the few ways of saving psychological fiction from pedagogical abstractness, and perhaps the best way to convey (rather than "explain") a conflict between conscious and unconscious energies. The problem for the novelist is to keep his narrator (or Jamesian "fool" and observer) self-deluded, imperceptive, blind; incapable of accurate self-analysis—yet have that narrator supply all the evidence necessary to the reader's understanding. He must say enough to convey his daily suffering and betray his true difficulties, but not say too much more.

Critics have more and more come to realize that a novelist's "technique" has some intimate relationship with his understanding of his characters, as well as a more obvious bearing on the mobility, energy, and persuasive-

* For Gide's intellectual conclusions at this time, we must look to the "Lettres à Angèle" (*OC*, III, 222–241). In 1898 Gide failed to distinguish clearly between the final affirmation of Nietzsche and the final renunciation of Dostoevsky, and brought them too close together by verbal legerdemain. If the individualist's energies are stifled, they may break out in some violent antisocial way. A universally accepted individualism, on the other hand, would ruin both the strong and the weak. The true "exceptional" man would be lost in the crowd of "meaningless eccentrics." There is no rule of thumb, Gide observes, by which we may distinguish the successes from the failures, the Nietzsches from the Stirners. We should therefore repudiate "individualism," out of respect for the individualist. Gide argued in much the same terms during his communist period.

ness of his books. But it is nearly impossible to demonstrate these relationships specifically, and even discussions of "point of view" are often disappointingly vague. The device of the obtuse narrator or observer is, however, a particular and definable one, and Gide's major success in using it deserves close analysis. *L'Immoraliste* also demands extensive comparison with other novels, short novels especially. *Great Expectations* prolongs a central imperceptiveness over many hundreds of pages, but does so primarily for dramatic suspense. The technique (which demands unusual and continued alertness on the reader's part) seems particularly suited to the short novel. To measure Gide's success in exploiting this "point of view" we should look to certain familiar short novels of Melville and of Joseph Conrad and Thomas Mann. How did they, faced by such a problem as Gide's, exploit the resources of this technique? The comparisons may seem digressive, but only such comparisons can establish *L'Immoraliste* in its proper place as one of the formal triumphs of the modern novel.

Melville's *Benito Cereno* is certainly one of the more conspicuous successes. Captain Delano is literally a "fool," wholly incapable of interpreting experience or of seeing evil, because of his benign temperament and Emersonian optimism. But for various reasons his story had to be more diffuse than Michel's. Melville wanted to involve the reader in Delano's error, and not merely for the sake of suspense or melodramatic surprise. "You too, optimistic and complacent reader," he might have said; "this is the way you too would have calumniated innocence and rationalized evil!" Following such an intention, and conceiving such a drama of appearance and reality, Melville had to provide much misleading or irrelevant appearance. His grave prose rhythms and mortuary similes promise tragedy, but the reader has little opportunity to detect what this tragedy will be. Only the long legal deposition fully corrects Delano's distortions and reconstructs the events in detail. It provides a retrospective irony and horror, and ultimately proves that even the truth cannot shatter Delano's optimism. The deposition is very effective in its cold phraseology and abstract

117

summation of death; only the lazy reader would want to see it go. But it suggests one of the ways in which the technique of the obtuse narrator or observer may thwart economy.

Dostoevsky, of course, provides several close analogues. *The Gambler* is as autobiographical as *L'Immoraliste,* but offers a much slighter separation of the character's consciousness from that of the author—who, incidentally, returned to his compulsive gambling immediately after finishing his book. *The Double,* however, dramatizes an unconscious conflict with great care, and anticipates the Freudian categories astoundingly: Golyadkin, Sr., as the menaced ego, while Golyadkin, Jr., acts out in turn the obscene id, the successful ego-ideal, and the accusing superego. *The Double* is nevertheless the story of a neurotic descending into psychosis, as the early visit to the doctor warns us. Thus an alert reader separates himself from the character almost at once and accepts no evidence at face value. But in *Notes from Underground* Dostoevsky undertook a formal task very similar to Gide's. Like Gide, he understood that his narrator was neurotic, yet he shared some of his feelings and attitudes: his hatred of deterministic psychology and his longing to act gratuitously, his disgust with positivist ethics. The problem was to write a psychological novel which would yet raise certain ideas provocatively. But Dostoevsky's blending of the two interests was less satisfactory than Gide's. The isolated and self-destructive "underground mouse," compelled to reënact a few experiences of childhood and adolescent rejection, does not understand why he acts as he does. He long bemuses us with his circular diatribe against determinism, but this essay is really irrelevant.

Five pages—and five pages more clearly dissociating author and subject—would have sufficed. For it is the body of the novel that proves man can act against his own interests, and does so not freely but compulsively. In this second part too, the formal difference from *L'Immoraliste* is enormous. Dostoevsky offers us not only obtuseness but the "original," chaotic, diffuse experience of the neurotic. He gives the full stenographic report of a patient's confession—from which we may, if we are sufficiently alert, deduce our clear conclusions. And there is much evidence that Dostoevsky knew he was doing just this. The narrator is diffuse only when what he says is irrelevant. He reveals the important facts of his story (his schoolboy experiences, for instance, or his onanism) in begrudging, bitter, and very brief asides. Thus *Notes from Underground* is in one sense a more authentic "report" than *L'Immoraliste,* and certainly takes us closer to the lived experience of neurotic suffering, the actual impression of hourly damnation. But for these very reasons it may offer less psychological understanding and achieve a rarer impression of tragedy. Tragedy is not mere suffering, but suffering delimited and ordered, understood with finality.

Conrad's *Heart of Darkness* has much of *Benito Cereno*'s density of atmosphere and calculated ambiguity of appearance, and at times it may recall the evasiveness of *Notes from Underground.* The author's purpose here as in his longer novels was to involve the reader minutely, and at whatever tiring of his patience. But other short novels by Conrad, told in the first person or seen by an obtuse observer, show an economy as impressive as Gide's. Conrad's general impulse was the same: to dramatize compulsive inward journeys, the very processes of self-exploration and self-discovery. And he too dramatizes unconscious identification—Marlow allying himself with the atavistic Kurtz, or the young captain of *The Secret Sharer* with the fugitive from the "Sephora," or the crew of the "Narcissus" with the malingering James Wait. But only *The Smile of Fortune* presents the kind of sexual self-delusion which would have interested Gide, and did interest him in *Isabelle.* Conrad's usual practice was to universalize such particulars and to see the conflict with the unconscious or preconscious in large symbolic terms. A few very slight changes could give *The Secret Sharer* a localized and even homosexual meaning. But the story as it stands has no such primary meaning. The captain's double is instead the whole of the unconscious, to be explored and recognized—including that area of the unconscious which may provoke unreflective action and unpremeditated crime. Technically, *The Secret Sharer*

119

shows the same formal control as *L'Immoraliste*. The narrator describes an experience of extreme incoherence, and even manages to convey a state of mind bordering on madness. Yet his cool report, like Michel's, contains very little that is irrelevant. It seems to move with the casualness and waste of unselective realism, but nearly every word counts. Much of Conrad's success here, and in the still more generalized *Shadow-Line,* lies in his full evocation of a plausible speaking voice. This is also one of the reasons for Gide's success with Michel. Extreme economy of narrative is masked by these calm and casual tones.

The closest approach to Gide's novel, in subject and technique, is Thomas Mann's *Death in Venice,* which was written a few years later. It is essentially the same story of latent and unrecognized homosexuality leading to self-destruction—though the reader who finds only theorizing on individualism in Gide may find only theorizing on the artist in Mann. Like Michel, Gustav von Aschenbach goes on a journey, not realizing that it is a journey within nor understanding the reasons for his restlessness. He too pays severely for his years of discipline and excessive restraint. The same alternating impulses to concentrate and to dissolve the self-control these two destinies, and both men—frightened by their new anarchy—make one last strong effort to recover self-control. Both rationalize their aggressive inward drives in philosophical terms. But their real objective is the restraining superego, which must be destroyed before Tadzio and Ali can be enjoyed. Gustav von Aschenbach's homosexual reactions are fewer than Michel's, though Mann had read Freud and Gide had not. Mann's hero is repelled by the old and painted homosexual on the boat from Pola to Venice, that exact image of his future self, as Michel is repelled for a time by Ménalque. But his most characteristic pederast reaction—a delighted recognition that Tadzio will die young *and therefore never be a mature man*—comes later in the story than Michel's resentment of Charles's growing-up. The two men are most strikingly alike in the way they externalize their inward conflicts. Michel's frenzied effort to probe and uncover the secrets of the Heurtevents is a symbolic attempt to uncover his own secret. In precisely the same way Gustav von Aschenbach, only dimly aware of his inner plague, combats the efforts of the Venetian authorities to conceal the cholera epidemic (after a brief period of pleased complicity). These things, all things, must be brought to the surface.

We have thus the same minute drama of self-delusion and self-discovery, and roughly the same separation between the author's consciousness and his character's. The great initial difference is that Michel is an obtuse narrator and Gustav von Aschenbach an obtuse observer, whose observations are rephrased by the author's ironic detachment. But the separation is at first unclear. How much of this sophisticated weary irony (and how many of these reflections on the "artist") are shared by Mann and Gustav von Aschenbach? Mann's technique most closely resembles Gide's after Tadzio has entered the story. At this point we are offered ample evidence of the latent homosexuality. But Mann does not "explain" why Gustav von Aschenbach acts as he does until the victim can explain it himself. Both stories, incidentally, show the same technical flaw. These wholly inward stories need no outside pressures to achieve their tragic ends. Yet Mann brings in an outside force—the misdirection of the baggage—to "tip the scales toward anarchy," as Gide brings in Ménalque. Of the two, Gide's mistake is the more serious one. For it suggests that Michel's inward debate needed pedagogical support from without.

These are some of the resemblances. But there are differences in conception, which are reflected closely in structure and technique. *L'Immoraliste* is the purer Freudian drama of the two, since both the homosexual urge and the tyrannical repressive force long remain unconscious. But in *Death in Venice* the restraining force is often conscious—a conscious longing for dignity and order— and the hero is not merely an intellectual but himself a psychological novelist. No doubt he too could interpret his love of the ocean as a yearning "for the unorganized, the immeasurable, the eternal—in short, for nothingness." His more conscious struggle therefore demands more explicit analysis than Michel's—even though much of that analysis may be deliberately misleading.

Beyond this, Mann offers a grand over-all "explanation" which Gustav von Aschenbach could not have made. This is the four-part equation of homosexuality, plague, unconsciousness, and death; the hero approaching one is approaching them all. Thus the daydream in Munich anticipates that atavistic dream in Venice which "left the whole cultural structure of a lifetime trampled on, ravaged, and destroyed." And the tiger in the bamboo thicket of the daydream is a real tiger in the "primeval island-jungle" of the Ganges Delta where the cholera epidemic began. Here already the author has "added something" to nature, for the sake of explanation and for dramatic effect. But how much more he adds in the occult appearance of the three strangers: the man standing near the funeral hall in Munich; the lawless gondolier with his gondola black as a coffin; the entertainer with his homosexual gestures, his unprovoked hysteria, and his heavy carbolic smell. For Gustav von Aschenbach does not see what author and reader see—that they are the same man, with the same facial characteristics, alike beckoning the hero to self-discovery, unconsciousness, and death. They are, simply, his destiny.

The texture of *Death in Venice* is realistic—and Mann, like Melville and Dostoevsky, offers a great deal of irrelevant detail (the description of Tadzio's sisters, for instance) to make his story more plausible. But the over-all structure is symbolist in a manner as traditional as Chaucer's in *The Pardoner's Tale*. *L'Immoraliste* confines itself, instead, to our only too natural world. Against the ingenious symbolist connections of *Death in Venice* it offers the structural firmness and inward connections of a fully dramatized psychic situation. Most obvious are the falling then rising line of Michel's health, as Marceline's line rises and declines; the balance of the two visits to La Morinière as Michel preserves then destroys his estate, and the vast circular movement from Biskra back to Biskra. Even these unities (if we accept the common view that tuberculosis is often a neurotic illness) seem psychologically necessary. More specifically, each step in Michel's journey looks forward to some future step: the fight with the drunken coachman near Positano to the kissing of the coachman in Taormina; the gardens of Biskra to the gardens of Ravello; the daylight rides with Charles to the nighttime poaching with Alcide. Yet these anticipations are never fortuitous, as the gondolier's anticipation of the entertainer is fortuitous. The changed Michel is compelled to return to the same places and experiences, if only to discover how he has changed.

Still more challenging, to the student of realism, is the fact that nearly everything Michel says and nearly everything he sees has a direct bearing on his sexual problem. He keeps Moktir's theft secret not merely because he sees in it an acting-out of his own longing to rebel against accepted decencies, but because he here enters into a first clandestine relationship with a child. A large psychological situation is thus perfectly dramatized in the action or inaction of a moment; the "gratuitous act" of sympathetic identification is in no sense gratuitous. Yet Michel's prolonged compulsive need to spend all his money is, to the reader of Menninger and Freud, fully as convincing. The novel offers very little "neutral" or innocent imagery. Lassif's canals and Lachmi's gourd for collecting the sap from palm trees are images as primary, for this latent homosexual, as the eels he caught with Charles; clay and shrub alike have a fleshy texture. How could Gide, using so much significant imagery, yet contrive to give an impression of real life, of unselected experience? The question poses itself when we recall the amount of "wasted" imagery in Mann and Dostoevsky, wasted for the sake of realism. One answer is that Gide's significant images also serve as casual images—*and so serve because never explained.* No single image or experience, but the cumulative effect of them all, drives us very slowly to an awareness of Michel's trouble. Everything in Michel's story leads to his revelation in the last line, yet no particular page seems to lead there in an obvious way. The minutiae of style and technique thus disguise an economy as extreme as any in modern fiction. Could Gide achieve a latent homosexual's vision of experience so exactly and so economically only because he had been, himself, a latent homosexual? To ask this is to take a very naïve view of the art of fiction—and to forget the imperfections of certain earlier books. In *L'Immoraliste* he reduced a most confused personal experience to an order which even the best-adjusted writers rarely achieve.

It is hardly the intention of this book to defend realism as such, and the anti-realism of *Les Faux-Monnayeurs* may have done more for the modern novel. But *L'Immoraliste* is a great realistic novel, and perhaps the best novel Gide would write. It demanded a fairly extended analysis because it shows us, at the outset, the characteristic tactics and strategy of Gide's other *"récits."* Beyond this it proves that even the realistic and subjective psychological novel may be economical. The neurotic experience of a Michel can be more than neurotic experience; it can reflect a universal conflict. And it requires, to be told, neither the diffuseness of *Notes from Underground,* nor the confusion of *The Double,* nor the superimposed intellectualism of *Death in Venice.* These are great works, and perhaps more astonishing at a first reading than *L'Immoraliste.* But Gide's novel belongs with them. And, like a great poem, it deserves and can survive repeated readings.*

Albert J. Guerard

---

* From *André Gide,* Harvard University Press, 1951, 2nd ed., with new material, 1969. Quotations are from the Dorothy Bussy 1930 translation.

Two Dissenting Opinions on
The Immoralist

ANDRÉ GIDE

The Afterword is essentially unchanged from the critique
Gide read in manuscript, and on which he commented in
a letter of May 16, 1947. The reaction seems touchingly
that of a parent who wants none of his children praised
at the expense of the others. Moreover, a writer of
seventy-seven (still active in spite of what he says below)
may resent having a work completed over forty-five years
before thus singled out. Above all, *The Immoralist* was
based on a phase of life Gide was willing to look back
on, courageously even, but of which he was hardly
proud. Contrition and guilt remain strong in the posthu-
mously published account of his honeymoon *(Madeleine)*.
To praise *The Immoralist* over such an inventive work
as *Les Caves du Vatican* might thus seem tantamount to
praising guilty personal experience over hard-won imaginative creation.

I would reply that no imaginative creation could be
more hard-won than *The Immoralist,* no controlled transformation of life more remarkable. But here, translated,
is Gide's comment:

"As for my own work, I remain astonished by the
knowledge you have achieved, not only of my *récits,* but
of all the rest. Had I been able to read this study of my
books (absurd supposition!) before having written them,
what profit would I not have drawn from it! But now
that the game has been played, won or lost, and altogether withdrawn from the game, I detach myself from
it and do not know too much what to think. At each
praise or blame, I say to myself: the critic is perhaps
right. Only manifest errors or malignly tendentious in-
terpretations still startle me [*sursauter*]. I was startled only
once in reading you: in connection with the extraordinary
case you make for my *Immoralist,* the book to which you
accord your major praise. Can it be that you are really
right? Perhaps, perhaps. Nevertheless, I am astonished.

125

I know that some readers, but very rare ones, share your opinion: Louis Martin-Chauffier, for instance, who recently told me to what degree this book had overwhelmed [*bouleversé*] him. But how many other readers—and among the most important ones—were equally or even more overwhelmed by my *Porte étroite* (even Claudel!). If it were only a question of artistic success, I am not sure that the largest number of votes might not go to the *Symphonie pastorale* or to *Isabelle* (I speak here only of my short *récits*). At an extreme even my *École des femmes* was able to bring enthusiastic sympathies until then refused my other books. I tell you this, certainly not to protest your opinion, but because the *literary case* seems to me rather exceptional: that of an author, of whom this or that book is in turn judged the best or the most important. A number of my shrewdest readers have a marked predilection for *Paludes*. As for me, I cannot manage to consider my *Immoralist* as better than the others in any respect, literary, moral, psychological . . . However, what you say about its latent and precursive Freudianism seems to me very true and deserves to be taken into consideration."*

THOMAS MANN

Thomas Mann reviewed at great length my book on Gide (which contained in appendix Gide's letter quoted above) in the *New York Times Book Review*. This review now appears as an Introduction to the second and paper editions. It offers a fascinating and sympathetic response of one great sinuous writer to a contemporary even more sinuous and "demoralizing." Does my comparison of *The Immoralist* and the less economical *Death in Venice* account in part for Mann's unexpectedly severe comment on Gide's book? The section of the review concerned with *The Immoralist* is subjoined:

". . . Mr. Guerard quite correctly calls the author of

* The French text is published as an appendix in my book *André Gide* (Harvard University Press, 1951, 2nd ed., 1969), now available as a Dutton paperback.

126

The Immoralist, The Counterfeiters, and *The Vatican Swindle** (Knopf, 1925) one 'of the most important novelists of our century, and who has modified our ideas and our image of the modern world,' and he supports this statement chiefly with *The Immoralist,* to him Gide's best novel and one of the masterpieces of modern fiction. He puts this early work not only above the impudent, entertaining *The Vatican Swindle,* but above *The Counterfeiters.*

"It is not easy for me to concur with Mr. Guerard's judgment, which, incidentally, presents a somewhat humorous contradiction to the fact that it is *The Counterfeiters* to which Mr. Guerard dedicates, in his fourth chapter, the most extensive interpretation—the truly critical virtuoso piece of the book. Isn't *The Immoralist* of 1902 a first novel of rather faded originality, whose capacity to shock has largely been lost through the decades, and whose title, inspired by Nietzsche, smothers the content by sheer philosophical dead weight?

"And, after all, isn't it *The Counterfeiters* which plays a more important role in the history of the European novel than *The Immoralist?* And the name of André Gide, the novelist, won't it be rather connected with the great, experimental *Counterfeiters* of a man almost sixty? Today (and it has been like this for quite some time) we need more 'sense of history,' more distance from our actual knowledge of psychology—not to say sexual pathology—in order to appreciate the earlier work.

"True, long before Freud's research data had reached the public's consciousness, the story of *The Immoralist* anticipated a complete insight into the conflict between conscious and pre- or sub-conscious life. This insight stems from Gide's homosexual disposition—which remained latent and misunderstood for a surprisingly long time—a disposition which has been the root and fount of his moral dynamism, of his revolutionary disavowal of everything respectable-traditional, and of all conformist security. It has made him into a great mover and shaker who, in the long run, will have served human progress,

---

* *Les Caves du Vatican;* in America, *Lafcadio's Adventures.*

and who could say of himself: 'To disturb, that is my role.'

"In an admirable manner, Mr. Guerard puts into bold relief the basic procreative dilemma of this mind. He makes us experience this dilemma between an inherited puritanism, never denied and never to be denied, and the self-preservation of a natural drive that deviates from the so-called 'natural.' Incapable of both a nonchalant hedonism (which he pursued occasionally and made predominant in *The Fruits of the Earth*) and of an unfettered puritanism, this mind oscillates—or plays—between the realm of order, which he needs desperately, and that of anarchy, to which he is equally heir. Until at the end he makes this very state of oscillation the basis of a new ethics."

ABOUT THE AUTHOR

ANDRÉ GIDE was born in Paris in 1869 and died there in 1951. He was awarded the Nobel Prize for Literature in 1947. Besides *THE IMMORALIST,* his major works include *The Counterfeiters, Strait Is the Gate, The Cellars of the Vatican,* and his three volumes of *Journals.* He also wrote plays, essays, short stories and books of travel.

THE NAMES THAT SPELL GREAT LITERATURE

Choose from today's most renowned world authors—every one an important addition to your personal library.

Hermann Hesse

☐	BENEATH THE WHEEL	2509 •	$1.50
☐	MAGISTER LUDI	2645 •	$1.75
☐	DEMIAN	2944 •	$1.75
☐	NARCISSUS AND GOLDMUND	6891 •	$1.75
☐	ROSSHALDE	7370 •	$1.50
☐	STEPPENWOLF	7979 •	$1.50
☐	GERTRUDE	10060 •	$1.95
☐	THE JOURNEY TO THE EAST	10136 •	$1.75
☐	SIDDHARTHA	10266 •	$1.75

Alexander Solzhenitsyn

☐	AUGUST 1914	2997 •	$2.50
☐	ONE DAY IN THE LIFE OF IVAN DENISOVICH	2949 •	$1.50
☐	THE LOVE-GIRL AND THE INNOCENT	6600 •	$ .95
☐	STORIES AND PROSE POEMS	7409 •	$1.50
☐	CANCER WARD	8271 •	$1.75

Jerzy Kosinski

☐	BEING THERE	2265 •	$1.50
☐	STEPS	2597 •	$1.50
☐	THE DEVIL TREE	7865 •	$1.50
☐	THE PAINTED BIRD	8257 •	$1.75

Doris Lessing

☐	THE SUMMER BEFORE THE DARK	2640 •	$1.95
☐	THE GOLDEN NOTEBOOK	7747 •	$1.95
☐	THE FOUR-GATED CITY	7937 •	$1.95

André Schwarz-Bart

☐	THE LAST OF THE JUST	7708 •	$1.50
☐	A WOMAN NAMED SOLITUDE	7880 •	$1.75

Buy them at your local bookstore or use this handy coupon for ordering:

Bantam Books, Inc., Dept. EDG, 414 East Golf Road, Des Plaines, Ill. 60016

Please send me the books I have checked above. I am enclosing $_____
(please add 35¢ to cover postage and handling). Send check or money order—
no cash or C.O.D.'s please.

Mr/Mrs/Miss_____

Address_____

City_____State/Zip_____

EDG—8/76

Please allow three weeks for delivery. This offer expires 8/77.